OT

COMING SOON!

The Goddess of Forgetfulness
(Book 4, Immortal Matchmakers, Inc. Series)
Skinny Pants (Book 3, The Happy Pants Café Series)
Check (Part 3, Mr. Rook's Island Series)
Digging A Hole (Book 3, The Ohellno Series)

THE ACCIDENTALLY YOURS SERIES

(Paranormal Romance/Humor)
Accidentally in Love with…a God? (Book 1)
Accidentally Married to…a Vampire? (Book 2)
Sun God Seeks…Surrogate? (Book 3)
Accidentally…Evil? (a Novella) (Book 3.5) ← You are here. ☺
Vampires Need Not…Apply? (Book 4)
Accidentally…Cimil? (a Novella) (Book 4.5)
Accidentally…Over? (Series Finale) (Book 5)

THE FATE BOOK SERIES

(Standalones/New Adult Suspense/Humor)
Fate Book
Fate Book Two

THE FUGLY SERIES

(Standalones/Contemporary Romance)
fugly
it's a fugly life

THE HAPPY PANTS SERIES

(Standalones/Romantic Comedy)
The Happy Pants Café (Prequel)
Tailored for Trouble (Book 1)
Leather Pants (Book 2)
Skinny Pants (Book 3) SPRING 2018

IMMORTAL MATCHMAKERS, INC., SERIES

(Standalones/Paranormal/Humor)

The Immortal Matchmakers (Book 1)

Tommaso (Book 2)

God of Wine (Book 3)

The Goddess of Forgetfulness (Book 4) WINTER 2017

THE KING SERIES

(Dark Fantasy)

King's (Book 1)

King for a Day (Book 2)

King of Me (Book 3)

Mack (Book 4)

Ten Club (Series Finale, Book 5)

THE MERMEN TRILOGY

(Dark Fantasy)

Mermen (Book 1)

MerMadmen (Book 2)

MerCiless (Book 3)

MR. ROOK'S ISLAND SERIES

(Romantic Suspense)

Mr. Rook (Part 1)

Pawn (Part 2)

Check (Part 3) COMING 2018

THE OHELLNO SERIES

(Standalones/New Adult/Romantic Comedy)

Smart Tass (Book 1)

Oh Henry (Book 2)

Digging A Hole (Book 3) COMING 2018

Accidentally ...Evil?

An Accidentally Yours *Evil* Novella

BOOK 3.5 OF THE ACCIDENTALLY YOURS SERIES

MIMI JEAN PAMFILOFF

A Mimi Boutique Novel

Print Edition

Cover Design by Earthly Charms (www.earthlycharms.com)
Creative Editing by Latoya C. Smith (lcsliterary.com)
Proof Reading by Pauline Nolet (www.paulinenolet.com)
Formatting by bbebooksthailand.com

Like "Free" Pirated Books?

Then Ask Yourself This Question: WHO ARE THESE PEOPLE I'M HELPING?

What sort of person or organization would put up a website that uses stolen work (or encourages its users to share stolen work) in order to make money for themselves, either through website traffic or direct sales?

Haven't you ever wondered?

Putting up thousands of pirated books onto a website or creating those anonymous ebook file sharing sites takes time and resources. Quite a lot, actually.

So who are these people? Do you think they're decent, ethical people with good intentions? Why do they set up camp anonymously in countries where they can't easily be touched? And the money they make from advertising every time you go to their website, or through selling stolen work, **what are they using if for?**

The answer is you don't know.

They could be terrorists, organized criminals, or just greedy bastards. But one thing we DO know is that

THEY ARE CRIMINALS who don't care about you, your family, or me and mine.

And their intentions can't be good.

And every time you illegally share or download a book, YOU ARE HELPING these people. Meanwhile, people like me, who work to support a family and children, are left wondering why anyone would condone this.

So please, please ask yourself who YOU are HELPING when you support ebook piracy and then ask yourself who you are HURTING.

And for those who legally purchased/borrowed/obtained my work from a reputable retailer (not sure, just ask me!) muchas thank yous! You rock.

DEPARTMENT OF JUSTICE
FBI ANTI-PIRACY
WARNING
FIDELITY
BRAVERY
INTEGRITY
FEDERAL BUREAU OF INVESTIGATION

ACCIDENTALLY ...EVIL?

WARNING:

This book contains sexual content, many naughty words, a hot, seven-foot deity with unrealistically large physical characteristics, talking animals, silliness, snark, sarcasm, and blatant abuse of the English language. Hope you enjoy!

NOTE FROM CIMIL:

Ex-goddess of the Underworld

Hellooo there, my little people pets! I bet right now you're thinking, *what the heckity-heck is this novella nonsense?* I bet you want to know what happens next to our hunky ex-god Kinich. I bet you think I should be spanked for allowing Mimi to make you wait.

All right. Yes! That last one is all me.

As for the novella (aka narrative, short story, potboiler, yarn) there is something you don't know. Something important. Something dark. And our little Accidentally Yours, apocalyptic love-safari, including mine, cannot continue until you've heard the story of my brother Chaam, God of Male Virility. Because without a little bitterness, there can be no sweet. Without yin, no yang. Without flabby thighs, no disco Zumba. And then where, *where!* would you be, pray tell?

But I warn you, this sad sniffler of a tale is one of tragedy and sacrifice without an ending. (Yet.)

"What?" you say. "Another cliffhanger?"

Why, of course it is! Not even I, the great Ex-goddess of the Underworld, now domestic love slave to Roberto (aka Narmer, Bob the Ancient One, Crusty Old Pharaoh), knows exactly how this series will end. (Possibly.) I mean, it's impossible (not really) to believe that such a tangled mess will just simply work itself out in the end. Isn't it?

But what do I know? (Everything.) I'm useless without my dead to tell me the future…

TTFN,
Cimil
Lowly Scrubber of Immortal Tighty Whities and Other Assorted Vampire Garments

There has to be evil so that good
can prove its purity above it.

—Buddha

Chapter One

Bacalar, Mexico. November 1, 1934

Why is that man... naked?

Dazed and flat on her back, twenty-one-year-old Margaret O'Hare observed the man's bare backside as he stood on a nearby weather-beaten dock, toweling off. Her vision, at first a groggy mess, focused to a machete-sharp point, the pain in her forehead equally knifelike.

Yes. Naked. Really. Really. Naked. She'd never seen such a large well-built man or such a perfect backside—hard, deeply tanned, and worthy of a marble sculpture. Maybe two. Or five. Too bad she was a painter.

Hold on. Where the ham sandwich am I? Margaret's eyes, the only body part she could move without experiencing pain, whipsawed from side to side. *Jungle. Dirt. Lake. Okay. I'm lying near the lake.* Yes, this was good. She recognized the place. Sort of.

Am I near the village dock?

Her peripheral vision said no; this dock had a tiny palapa for shade at the very end.

Then where am I?

She made a feeble attempt to lift her throbbing head, but her body rewarded her with a spear to the temple.

Ow. Ow. Ow. She took a slow breath to allow the skull-shattering jab to dissipate. *All right. Relax and think. What happened? What happened? What happened? And who is Mr. Perfectbottom over there?*

A sticky blanket of gray coated her thoughts, but she did recall swimming that morning. Maybe she'd slipped on the village dock and fell into the lake. Maybe Mr. Perfectbottom had been bathing down at the shore and rescued her.

Or not.

Her clothes were bone-dry except for the sweaty parts. Come to think of it, she felt like a mud pie, soggy underneath and dry on top, baking in the sun. It didn't help that someone—maybe the man?—had placed a warm fur under her head and neck. God, it was itchy.

She willed her hand to make the painful journey behind her ear to give it a good scratch. Her fingers brushed the soft, silky hairs of the makeshift pillow.

How odd. People in these parts don't wear mink.

The mink coat purred.

Maggie sprang from the moist grass and scrambled back a few feet against a thick tree trunk. "Ja-ja-jaguar!"

The glossy black coated creature didn't budge a paw. It simply stared, its eyes reminding her of two big limes—wide, round, and green. Then the damned thing smiled right at her like some real-life Cheshire cat. Goddamned disturbing.

"You! Cat!" The man barreled down the dock, each heavy step thundering across the creaky wooden planks. "Leave! Do not return until I call you."

Maggie should have been frightened by the boom of the man's tone, but instead, his rich masculine timbre soothed her aching head.

"Raarrr?" the cat...

...responded? I must be hearing things, she thought, her eyes toggling back and forth between man and beast.

"Do as you are told," he said to the animal, "or the deal is off."

The black cat hissed, whipped its tail through the air, and dissolved into the shadows of the lush vegetation surrounding the small lakeside clearing.

This is too bizarre; I need to get out of here. Maggie turned her wobbling body to seek shelter in another dream.

"Where the *hell* do you think you're going?" said that deep, rich voice that wrapped her mind in ribbons of warm caramel and exotic spices.

Before she could mutter a word, her head cartwheeled and her body tipped. Two firm hands gripped her shoulders and propped her against the tree. "Close your eyes. Breathe."

She suddenly wanted to do just that. And only that. The man's voice was...compelling.

As she sucked in the thick tropical air, her mind slotted missing memories back into place. She recalled searching for the path to the ruin where her father spent his days. Little Kinichna'—or Little House of the Sun, as he called it—was the biggest find of his career, the one that would put his name on the archeologists' map. Ironically, the dilapidated and historically uninteresting pile of rubble had been known about for years, but when her father's colleague asked that he decipher etchings from a rare black jade tablet found not too far away, he'd realized they were directions, an ancient Mayan treasure map. Said map led to a hidden chamber right underneath Little Kinichna'.

"You are now well. Open your eyes," the man's husky voice commanded.

She took a moment to survey her body.

Miraculous. Her pain *was* gone. In fact, she felt downright euphoric and tingly. Especially in the spots where he touched her. Maybe in a few other spots, too. *Margaret O'Hare! You dirty trollop!*

She opened her lids, shocked to find two icy turquoise eyes just an inch from her face, their unfathomable depths filled with primal desire.

Applesauce! She jerked her head back and knocked it on the tree. "Ouch!" *Great. Now I have a lump on the back to match the front.*

The colossal man straightened his powerful frame and towered over her like a giant oak, but he didn't release her from his fierce gaze.

Well, at least he'd put a socially acceptable distance between their heads. The same could not be said for their bodies; the heat from his heaving chest seeped right through her. And thankfully—or was it regrettably?—or perhaps magically, since she didn't know how he'd had the time?—he now wore a pair of simple white linen trousers. No. It was a definite "thankful." The moment was awkward and unsettling enough without the man being naked *and* staring. Which he was. Studying her with his beautiful turquoise eyes dressed in a thick row of incredibly black lashes.

Why the deviled egg is he looking at me like that?

Maybe he thinks that giant lump on my forehead is about to give birth to an extra head.

"What happened?" she finally asked.

"I'll ask the questions, woman," he said. "Who are you?"

Not the response she'd expected. "Oh, ducky. I'm lost in the jungle with a half-naked rake."

"Rake?" Dark brows arching with irritation, he planted his arms—silky milk chocolate poured over bulging, never-ending ropes of taut muscle—across the hard slopes of his bare chest. Maggie meticulously cataloged the man's every divine detail, like she did for each precious artifact from her father's dig. He had long reams of shimmering midnight hair that fell over menacingly broad shoulders; the cords of muscles galloping down his bronzed neck into said broad shoulders; and his sinfully sculpted abdomen tightly divided into rounded little rectangles, which reminded her of an ice cube tray—a fancy new invention. *God, I miss ice cubes.*

But as impressive as his raw, abundantly masculine features were, it was his height that most bewildered her. People from these parts were not known for stature. In fact, at five feet six, she had a good six inches on the tallest men in the village, and her father, Dr. O'Hare, an entire foot. No. This giant man most certainly wasn't from the sleepy little pueblo of Bacalar or anywhere in the Yucatan, for that matter. But then, from where? His exotic, ethnically ambiguous features didn't provide any clues. He could be a Moroccan Greek Spaniard or a Nordic Himalayan Kazak. *Hmmm…*

"Yes, rake, as in cad? Or if you prefer, savage," she said.

"Hardly. Savages don't save women in distress. They create them."

True. They also don't have wildly seductive, exotic accents. Like one of her parents' Hollywood friends.

Lightbulb.

"Oh my God. You're a picture film actor, aren't you?"

Yes. Yes. It all made sense now. The locals in the village had been talking about a film crew for weeks. Word on the street—errr, word on pueblo corner next to the stinky burro—was that a famous Russian director was making a movie about Chichen Itza and filming historical reenactments in the area.

"An...actor." His icy, unsettling expression turned into a charming smile inspired by the devil himself. "Yes."

She sighed. "That explains the trained cat. Where's the crew?" She glanced over her shoulders.

"Crew. Errr." He raised his index finger as if to point somewhere, then dropped it. "My crew will be here in a few days."

"Getting into character! Right." Maggie had heard firsthand how actors prepared for their roles. Fascinating business. Of course, acting had never really interested her. Nothing that required work ever had, which was why she'd taken up painting when her parents pestered her to do something productive. Going to parties and dating famous, good-looking men apparently weren't worthy pursuits.

They were right. If only her mother had lived long enough for Maggie to tell her so.

"Now," he said, "will you tell me who *you* are?"

She held out her hand. "Miss Margaret O'Hare of Los Angeles."

"You are a very long way from home."

No. Really? "I'm here working with my father. He's a professor doing...ummm...research."

A teeny fib. Or two. Who's gonna know? Truthfully, her father wasn't researching doodly-squat; he was secretly excavating. And the "work" she was doing? It didn't amount to a hill of pinto beans; her father wouldn't let her anywhere near the sacred structure. "No place for a young lady," he'd said. Well, neither was this slightly lawless, revolution-ravaged Mexican village, where electricity was considered a luxury—as were beds, curling irons, and those blessed ice cubes.

And chicken coops. Don't forget the chicken coops. The village was plagued with wretched little packs of villainous roaming chickens. *Like tiny feathered banditos who leave their little caca-bombs all over the damned place.*

You'll survive. Some things are more important.

"Well, Miss Margaret O'Hare from Los Angeles, very pleased to meet you." The man bent his imposing frame, slid his remarkably-rough-for-an-actor palm into hers, and placed a lingering kiss atop her hand.

An exquisite jolt crashed through her, causing her to buck. She snapped the tingling appendage away. *Wow. That kiss could combust a lady's drawers like gunpowder. Poof! Flames. No drawers. Just like that.*

The residual heat continued spreading. *Please don't reach my drawers. Please don't reach my drawers…*

He frowned and dropped his hand. "So tell me, what were you doing in the jungle, Margaret?"

"Jungle?"

"Yes, you know that place where I found you unconscious. Barefoot. All alone. It has many trees and dangerous animals." He pointed over her shoulder at the lush forest filled with vine-covered trees that chirped and clicked with abundant life. "It's right behind you, if you've forgotten what it looks like."

"Yes. That." *Thinking, thinking, thinking.* She wiggled her bare toes in the mushy grass and looked out across the hypnotic turquoise waves of the lake. Funny how the man's eyes were the exact same color right down to their flecks of shimmering green.

An early afternoon breeze pushed a few dark locks of hair across her face. *Still thinking, thinking, thinking.* She brushed them away and then focused on the grass stains on the front of her white cotton dress. Darn it. She loved this dress, with its tiny hand-stitched red flowers along the hem. Her father had had it specially made along with a beautiful black stone pendant the week they'd arrived. He'd said the gifts were in celebration of his find; everything was exactly where he'd thought, including some mysterious, priceless treasure that would "change their lives." He'd said he couldn't wait to show her when the time came.

"I'm waiting," the man said with unfiltered impatience.

"Waiting. Oh, yes. I was in the jungle because..." *Still thinking...*

Fear. Yes, fear was the reason she'd been capering about. Her mother's recent death had left her plagued with the corrosive emotion. She feared she would never make right with her past. She feared opening her eyes to the present. She feared the future would bring only pain and suffering because eventually anyone she cared for would leave. Fear was like an irrational cancer that ate away at her rational soul.

It was why, when her father began acting peculiar back home—disappearing for weeks at a time, mumbling incoherently, obsessing over that tablet—she came to Mexico. She feared he might simply disappear in this untamed land, evaporate into nothing more than a collection of memories—just as her mother had.

And now she feared that she had failed; her father had not been seen for three days. But she didn't dare articulate this distressing, gloomy thought aloud.

"Because…I am a painter!" she said. "I went exploring for new scenery. I got turned around, and then that giant cat of yours appeared out of nowhere and chased me." She rubbed the gigantic lump on her forehead. "I fell and hit my head. You didn't happen to find my sandals, did you?"

One glorious turquoise eye ticked for the briefest moment. "Searching for scenery?"

"You don't believe me?"

He shook his head and grinned with a well-polished arrogance only found on the face of a Hollywood actor. She quickly wondered if he'd ever met her mother but then dismissed the thought. She didn't want to think about her mother; the pain was simply too fresh.

"No. I do not believe you," he stated dryly.

The nerve! "You did find me in the jungle, didn't you? Wasn't I unconscious?" She pointed to the large lump on her forehead. "And wearing this?"

"Yes, but I believe you were searching for something else."

Nosy rake. "Well, it's been a pleasure, Mr...." *Arrogant Nudesunbather? Mr. Nomanners Perfectbottom?*

"Backlum Chaam."

Backlum? What an odd—oh! He's in character. "Sure, Joe. Whatever blows your wig, but—"

"The name is not Joe, it's Chaam. I just said it."

Margaret blinked. *Deep, deep into character.*

"And I assure you, I do not wear a wig. This is my real hair." He gave his shiny black mane a proud tug.

"I meant—oh, never mind. Listen, it's been great, Mr. *Chaam,* but I gotta skedaddle; my father is probably wondering where I am." She wished. Her father was likely dead. Or injured.

Stay calm. You'll find the ruin. You'll find him...

If only she'd insisted on knowing exactly where the excavation site was hidden. Instead, she'd done what her father had asked—fearing his anger—and stayed near the village, spending her days painting, learning Spanish from the local children, or swimming with a friend she'd made: a young woman named Itzel who didn't speak a lick of English.

"Have a lovely afternoon." She flashed an awkward grin and turned toward the shoreline.

A firm grip pulled her back and twirled her around. Two powerful arms incarcerated her body and smashed her against an astonishingly firm, naked chest. His touch instantly ignited that gunpowder, and…

Combustion!

A wave of carnal heat ripped through her body. *Oh my God. Oh my God. Oh my Gooood…* Margaret felt her face turn a lascivious red. Beads of volcanic sweat seeped through her pores. Every muscle in her body wound up with merciless unchaste tension, like ropes anchoring a massive sail, a sail blowing her ship toward the most delicious place ever. And then…

Release.

Maggie braced herself on the man's bountiful biceps as the tension snapped and silent fireworks exploded throughout her body.

Oh my god. Had she just…had she really just…?

He cleared his throat. "Was it as good as it looked?"

She let out an exaggeratedly long breath. *What the flapdoodle?* "You're not an actor, are you?" she asked, unable to keep her voice from quivering.

He shook his head from side to side. "No. And you are no human."

Chapter Two

Chaam beamed at the enchanting brunette in his arms, who gazed up at him with her large dark eyes—eyes that contrasted the sunburnt, freckled cheeks of her striking face. Did she have any clue how long he'd waited, how long he'd held the silent, impossible wish for her in his cold heart?

Seventy thousand years.

Seventy.

Thousand.

That was how long the mere hope of her had kept his existence tolerable. And that was why he found it impossible to believe his impossible wish had been granted. The gods did not have mates. Period. That privilege belonged only to those of human origin. Hell, even vampires occasionally found a mate. Lucky bastards. But regardless of the facts, he'd always allowed himself the fantasy. And he'd envisioned her seventy thousand different ways: a delicately framed blonde with sea green eyes; a seductive black female with velvety waves of chocolate brown hair and eyes of hazel; a tall and athletic woman, a warrior, with olive skin and straight dark hair. He'd imagined her many ways, but he'd never once imagined Margaret. Not the exotic sort, yet sinfully feminine with a crisp intelligence and a disarming smile. And clearly the product of these new times with her very masculine-style independence.

She was perfect for him in every way.

Perhaps this explained why despite the impossibility of this female being his mate, his body and soul screamed she was his. *But perhaps she is mine? A miracle. A gift from the universe.* Why else had he been able to touch her? When he'd first stumbled across the unconscious beauty in the jungle, her dark hair tangled with twigs and leaves, he'd assumed she'd met her demise. But then he stroked her cheek, and she made a tiny moan. Yes. With pleasure. Actual pleasure from his touch. Humans normally winced, shrieked, or passed out. But this one moaned.

He must have stood there with his mouth gaping for ten entire minutes, studying her ripe full breasts pressing against the white cotton fabric of her dress. And those smooth, creamy thighs… He'd seen them as clear as a blazing hot day with her dress hiked up the way it was, revealing the lacy hemline of her silky undergarments. Then he'd noticed her lips. Like her plump breasts, they were full, juicy…just ripe for a kiss. He'd debated for one agonizing second before he dove in and sampled their sweetness. Once he did, his heart made that leap toward believing the unbelievable because the vision thrust upon him in that moment could not be a product of his imagination. He was never that creative. Could she be his missing piece? His mate?

Idiot. Gods do not have mates. Your mind is connecting dots that do not exist because you want to believe. A more rational explanation might be that she was a genetic anomaly, a human tolerant of his touch. *Or that she is not human at all.*

"Wha-what did you say?" she stammered.

"Drop the charade. I know you aren't human." He gave a playful little squeeze, and she wiggled against him. *Ummm...delicious.* He couldn't get enough of her sensual warmth.

"You're crazy." She thrashed her head from side to side. "Let me go!"

That wasn't going to happen. Whatever—whoever—she was, he had no plans to release her.

Yet.

She was simply too enticing. A tall, curvy drink of water after a seventy-thousand-year drought.

"Help! Help!" She clawed at his bare arms.

"I will let you go, little bobcat," he grunted, "if you promise not to run."

"I am *not* a bobcat! Help!"

"Okay, then. My little—" *saucy clawed minx? Feral cupcake? Chipmunk of lust?* "Hell, I was never skilled in the pet-names department. Can't I simply call you bobcat?"

She froze; hostility raged in her eyes. "No. You most certainly cannot call me bobcat!"

He turned his head to avoid her pounding fists. "Stop your assault. I'm not going to hurt you." No, he certainly didn't want that. He did, however, want to do other things to her. "I want you to tell me *what* you are. Then I will release you."

More screams.

There was only one solution.

Spank her?

No, idiot. Start with showing her the vision you saw upon discovering her. Perhaps this will entice her to answer. He dipped his head and kissed her softly. The woman stilled in his arms.

Yes, now she sees, too.

Words couldn't describe the deific enormity of the visions he shared. Stars, millions of stars, laughter and joy, the eternal thread of love weaving itself through every beam of sunlight, the divine spark of life in every drop of rain, the two of them lying naked under the tropical night sky. He had seen every step, every moment in time leading up to today.

Fate had brought them together. But as much as he wished for her to be his mate, the truth was undeniable: Gods did not have mates, and they certainly could not be intimate with humans—the gods' energy was far too powerful for any sustained, passion-filled, physical contact—which was ironic because humans were the only species they felt anything for.

Yet, like a miracle, here she was. Saucy little

claws and all. And he'd simply stumbled upon her. Just like that.

Perhaps she is a miracle, yes. But human, no. This kiss—wet, thirsty, unfiltered—was proof.

He pulled away, craving another glance of her exquisite face that included a tiny dimple in her right cheek and a sexy little mole just below her lip. She was utterly unique. She was utterly perfect. He couldn't help but beam. "You saw the vision, didn't you, my little...love guppy? And now you understand."

The speed of her nod was impeded by her shock. "Did you really just call me 'love guppy'?"

He cringed. He would try to sell her on 'bobcat' again later.

"Who are you?" She glowered.

"Not who. What." Chaam released her. "I am a god. In fact, I believe I am *your* god."

Maggie had no clue what was happening, but when the strange man kissed her lips, it felt like her body had been tossed into a volcano of sin. Sin laced with chaos and the absolute certainty she'd never woken up from that horrific bump on her head.

The kiss made her see things, impossible things—him fighting alongside a swarm of savage men donning breastplates and swords, and later, sailing on a vessel from the days of Hernan Cortez. Whoever this man was, she hadn't a clue, but the bizarre shower of images was incredibly detailed.

She shook her head, trying to reorganize the

jumbled mess inside. "You really think you're... *God*?"

His eyes flickered from turquoise to gray. Or had she imagined it?

"God? Good heavens, woman, no. I said 'a god'—as in one of fourteen. I am the God of Male Virility."

Great. Mr. Hallucination-inducing Perfectbottom thinks he's the god of sexual prowess. That's far less zany than believing he's God.

"And you're telling me there are more of you?" she asked.

"Yes. This is what I said," he replied as if no one had ever questioned him. "Of course, every culture gives us different names—for example, the Egyptians called me Mir; the Greek, Eros; the Aztecs, Huehuecototl-Coyotlinahual."

"Hewy, hewy what?"

He pushed his wide shoulders back and puffed out his broad chest. "Huehue is Nahuatl for 'very old.' I am a Bacab—one of the first gods to be created, which means I am also one of the most powerful."

Suuure, Joe. She began pinching her arm. *Wake up. Wake up. Wake up.*

He placed his hand over hers. "Please do not do that. It is very disturbing."

"Disturbing. I'm disturbing *you*?"

He raised one dark brow. "Yes. That is what I said."

"But-gaaah-uhhhh."

"Now, tell me what you are," he said.

Her thoughts continued to stall and sputter like last year's Model B Ford. "I-I told you, I'm Margret O'Hare. I'm here assisting my father, who's doing field research on the Mayans."

Mr. Chaam dipped his head and stared deeply into her eyes, like a wolf sizing up its prey. "You are lying. I can see it. Why do you not trust me when you've seen the vision?"

The only thing Maggie trusted was that her marbles had gone on marble holiday to the marble Hamptons, where they were sipping teeny tiny marble martinis.

"What vision? I have no idea what you're talking about," she lied once again.

"Fine." He turned to leave. "If this is how you wish to proceed."

"Where are you going?" *And why do I care?* She trotted behind him. Though he wore no shoes—*look at those feet. Are those little muscles on those toes?*—he moved swiftly over the pebble-covered shoreline. "Hey, I asked you a question."

He abruptly stopped and turned. His intimidating height staggered her back. "I answer to no one," he said. "And let us always be clear on this point: My kind gives the orders, and right now, I am ordering you to stay here and await my return."

Yes. It was official. She'd hit her head and landed on Planet Pighead. And, "My kind"? Did he seriously believe he was a god? Then again that vision was…

She shook her head. "What is happening?"

Chaam took two wide steps forward and lifted her chin. "You are very cunning, Margaret O'Hare, but make no mistake, I am not the sort of god who enjoys playing games. When I return, you will tell me everything—who and what you are—then we shall spend the evening making love."

Maggie's knees knocked, nearly causing her to fall over. "We will do no such thing!"

He leaned down. "Fine," his hot breath tickled her ear as he whispered, "then it will be hard, hot fucking. Your choice."

Margaret gasped and stepped away. "What kind of woman do you think I am?"

A crooked smile leapt across his full lips. "The kind," he said all too slowly with that rich, syrupy voice infused with sex, "who will enjoy all that I have to offer. In fact, I'll wager that you'll be begging me for it." He glanced at his groin, which displayed the unmistakable outline of a rather large, slightly firmed penis.

Okay, maybe—What? Maggie! "You're disgusting. Never," she replied to him. Or possibly to herself. Who knew what was what at this point?

Chaam laughed with a deep, soul-felt chuckle. "Such strong words from a woman who orgasmed from my touch. Maybe you require another taste?" He grabbed her by the shoulders and kissed her hard. Just like before, her body coiled with tension, but he briskly released her before the wave of combustion took hold.

Regardless, she melted on the inside, becoming a lusty heap of loosely joined skin and bones.

He flashed a smug smile and continued down the shoreline with a victorious swagger. "Like you," he called out, "I have no idea what the hell is going on, but unlike you, I'm wise enough not to question." He stopped and looked at her with those piercing turquoise eyes. "I have suffered thousands of years watching others enjoy the exquisite delights of the flesh, and it is finally my turn. I will be inside you tonight, Margaret O'Hare. Fate has demanded it be so. You cannot fight fate." He shrugged happily and continued walking away.

The moments ticked by before she scrounged up a coherent thought. "You're a madman," she screamed, "if you think Maggie O'Hare is going to stand here waiting for you to return!"

"I would never be so foolish," he called out, not bothering to turn around or stop, "to underestimate a determined, headstrong woman such as yourself." He snapped his fingers.

The black jaguar appeared from the brush at Maggie's side. "Raaar?"

Oh, hell!

"Women." Chuckling, Chaam shook his head and kicked a few pebbles into the water. Didn't matter which species, they were all the same.

Stubborn, petty, and stubborn.

And mine. He stopped in his tracks. *Holy saints. Mine.* He still couldn't believe it, but the vision clearly showed they were destined to make love tonight. *Thank the gods, but what does it all mean?*

Perhaps, he supposed, she was the Creators' reward for many millennia of hard work. Yes. Gods save him, but his existence was a tedious one. One that required he ensure everyone—excluding himself or the other gods—had sex. He was even obliged to help the animals. After all, if they did not propagate, humans certainly wouldn't survive. But to make matters worse, his brethren held no respect for him. They called him His Holy Horndog and Deity of the Dick. Didn't they know sex was the necessary ingredient to cement the bond between two souls?

The epiphany hit him hard.

Yes, that was it! The answer. He would make love to her tonight. If she was his mate, their souls would unite. He would feel the powerful connection.

So simple.

He smiled brightly until another thought, this one dismal, smacked him upside the head like a cold brick. Whether or not she was his mate, he realized he could not keep her. He simply had no way to do so. His bond with the universe compelled him to serve humanity. That meant he traveled years at a time to the most remote corners of the world, sometimes by foot or by horse. When he did not travel, he aided humans with less severe issues from the comfort of his realm.

Christ, the universe is so damned cruel.

Suddenly, he hoped she was not his mate; it was one thing to suffer an eternity hoping for her, but it would be an unfathomable torment to have found her and always be separated. He could not stomach the thought.

His heart sank into a deep, dark hole.

Yes, as painfully disappointing as it might be, he hoped she was simply a human immune to his touch. Or, perhaps, not human at all. In either case, he prayed she was a woman he could walk away from.

He rubbed his face with both hands. *Christ, you're in deep shit.* He already knew that walking away from Maggie—mate or no mate—wasn't likely to happen. He wanted to keep her.

All right, man. You're a fucking deity. You've faced far worse, and you'll figure this out.

Unfortunately, he had a few errands to complete—a confused bull who enjoyed making it with a bush, a cricket who favored ladybugs—so, so disturbing—and a twenty-year-old human male who had met his soul mate, but hyperventilated and passed out every time she came near. Yes, he would quickly do his magic and then gather supplies for his own magical evening with…

My woman. Gods, he loved the sound of that.

For the first time in Chaam's entire existence, he smiled a smile that touched his soul.

Chapter Three

Maggie stood on the dock, swapping out two equally weighty emotions: fury and her old friend fear. Fury over being trapped by this madman and fear because her father was still missing.

Son of a biscuit! This couldn't be happening. At her mother's funeral, she'd silently promised to whoever was up there listening that she'd take care of him. It was the one damned thing she'd sworn to do, a commitment she would finally keep. Yes, her past was littered with broken promises. Promises to the men she'd dated—to seriously consider their offers; promises she'd made to herself—to stop being afraid of commitment; but mostly, promises to her mother—to try harder and make something of her life. It wasn't that she hadn't cared or respected herself, but Maggie simply never understood the point to any of it. "Life is precious and fleeting, Margaret," her mother would say. "Find your passion and the one thing you were born to do. Out of that, you'll find happiness and bring joy to others." Maggie simply didn't believe she had anything special to give, so she absorbed herself in passing the time. But when she'd sat at the funeral, looking out across a sea of faces who'd adored her mother, Maggie finally got why trying mattered. But that didn't make opening her heart to others, as her mother had done so freely, any easier. In fact, it was just the opposite. Now Maggie cared too much. And *that* was the reason she clung to her father. That was also the reason she couldn't stomach letting anyone else in. It hurt too much to lose.

Yes, and because of this, you will never fall in love. You will never commit to a man. Face it: you were born broken.

Then why are you feeling so strongly for—

"Well, hellooo there, cutie pie!"

Gah! Maggie jumped like a Mexican bean on the creaky dock. The tiny redhead had popped out of nowhere.

"You scared the lunch noodle out of me, lady." Maggie clutched a fist over her heart. "Where did you come from?"

It registered that the woman was wet and nude. *Could this day become any stranger? Or more naked?*

The crazed nudist wiggled her shoulders. "Obviously, I came out of the lake, sugar. Where else? Hey! Why are you on the dock, facing off with *The Jungle Book*? You must be a fan of anthropomorphic tales! Get it! Tales! Anthropomorphic!" The woman chortled and pointed at the gaggle of assorted animals now perched on the mouth of the dock—that enormous jaguar, a tiny furry pig of some sort, a black and white striped monkey, a bright green parrot, and, yes, to make the ensemble complete, a three-foot-long iguana.

Each time Maggie attempted to move in their direction, toward land or into the lake, the animals barked, hissed, and growled. Or snorted. Lots of snorting from the little pig thing.

Like she'd thought, could the day possibly get any stranger? And yes, anthropomorphic?

"To answer your second ridiculous question," said the redhead, "of course I know I'm naked. Really now, who wears clothes when they're in a lake? That would be just weird. Fish don't wear clothes, do they? On second thought!" She cackled and then doubled over. "That would be so cute! I love the idea. I'll have Sven, my tailor, make a bunch of miniature tuxedos. Boom! Fish-edos!"

The woman is out of her ever-loving, nudist screwball mind.

Well, crazy or not, Maggie needed help. She had to get off that dock before the man with those excessively large muscles and hot, mind-altering kisses returned. Maggie's drawers could only take so much before they'd disintegrate, her virtue and sanity right along with them.

The odd woman's laughter took a sudden nosedive and crashed. "Hey," she whispered, looking over both shoulders, "did you happen to see my brother? He's about yea so tall." She reached for the sky on her tippy toes.

That was when Maggie also noticed the woman's glowing turquoise eyes.

Heavens to Betsy, she's his sister? It made sense. So much goddamned sense.

Maggie pointed south down the shoreline. "He went thataway."

"Fabulous!" The screwball sauntered past Maggie toward the critters, who shrank back.

This was Maggie's chance. She took two steps forward, but the woman turned.

"Uh-uh-uhhhh," she sang out, wagging her pale index finger at Maggie. "You're staying put."

"But you can't leave me here."

The woman hee-hawed like a broken donkey. "Oh yes I can, sugar. Because this is your stage and you're the star of the show. The catalyst. The spark. The *fizzzz* in the gin fizzy. Ain't no party without you."

"What do you mean?"

"I don't have time to explain, doll, but trust me, you and I are going to have loads of time to catch up later."

"Huh?" said Maggie.

"You'll see. And don't forget, when the time comes, be sure to follow Chaam. He's your secret sauce."

"Sauce?"

"You know. The bom in your bomb-bomp-bom-bomp, the ram in your rama-lama-ding-dong."

The word *screwball* wouldn't do. No. Not at all.

"Ta-ta!" The woman waved her hand and

skipped down the shore. "And don't forget," she called out, "humankind will thank you later!"

Bat-shit crazy. Yes, that's it.

Three hours later

Chaam's heart quickened when he neared the lakeside clearing where he'd left Maggie. The "male therapy sessions" had gone rather well, with the exception of the cricket that insisted ladybugs were the "bee's knees," some strange bug code for "sexy." But once he pulled out the big guns—an unbreakable command that embedded itself in the male's subconscious—all was well in Cricket-ville. He then went to the pueblo's small *mercado* and found everything he needed for his special evening, including a bottle of Spanish wine and a matrimonial-sized hammock. The local seamstress had even made him a new linen shirt, right on the spot. Ah, it was good to be the God of Male Virility. Women tripped over themselves to please him.

But not Maggie. No. She was different.

He liked that.

As the sun shed its final rays, Chaam rounded the last small peninsula standing between him and his Maggie. His heart stumbled like a clumsy runner.

Maggie sat on the edge of the dock, dainty feet dangling in the lake, her long brown hair flowing down her back like a mystical Greek siren's. Her body, a curvy and voluptuous little package, embodied every feminine characteristic he adored.

Oh hell. He looked down at his dauntingly large erection. He'd be forced to take another dip in the lake to cool off, as he'd done three times earlier in the day while he'd been waiting for Maggie to wake.

Or, perhaps, I just needed to see...that. Chaam cringed.

Maggie scowled at the giant predator sitting a few yards away, guarding her like a juicy lamb chop. A half-dozen other animals had joined in the fun.

Chaam marched to the mouth of the dock. "I asked you to keep an eye on her, not have a party."

The cat made a little hiss, followed by random noises from the monkey, iguana, parrot, and pygmy hog.

Chaam crossed his arms and glared at the little pig. "You're on the wrong continent. You know that, don't you?"

Snort.

"Go!" Chaam barked. "All of you. I don't have time for this." He pointed to the small furry pig. "And you! Don't bother returning; I don't even speak pygmy hog!"

Chaam noticed Maggie staring with an expression somewhere between horror and...well, horror.

Chaam glanced back at the cat. It hadn't budged a stubborn furry inch. "Fine. Get them out of here, and I will help you tomorrow."

The cat smiled—Chaam hated that; it looked so wrong when animals smiled—and quickly disappeared with his entourage.

Maggie cleared her throat and lifted her chin. "Nice of you to return, Backlum—"

"Chaam. I go by Chaam."

"Savage! That's what I'll call you! How dare you! I'm leaving, and don't you dare try to stop me!"

"You will stay." He blocked her from passing.

"Or what?"

A mosquito the size of a small rodent perched on her cheek, and without thinking, Chaam swatted it.

"Ouch!" Maggie fell to the side and cupped her cheek.

Oh, Christ! He'd slapped her! Hard.

He quickly reached for her, but she shrunk back.

"I should have guessed," she hissed. "You cad!"

"No! There was a—"

"You can slap me around all you want," Maggie stood and closed the gap between them, "but you will never, ever have me. I'll die before I let you put another hand on me."

Chaam growled with frustration. Dammit! This was not how he'd imagined this special evening would begin.

The madman had slapped her. Actually slapped her! And then he growled! Like a goddamned beast.

And if he was capable of hitting her to gain submission, then, without a doubt, she was in danger.

Maggie stepped back and attempted to ignore how the man smelled. Incredible. Like sweet herbs mixed with something dark and dangerous.

Anise, fennel, black licorice! God, I want a bite. Or a lick. Or a nibble.

Oh, horse pucky. Being near him triggered a lapse in sanity—an added bonus to the danger equation.

Yes, but that vision. That kiss.

He hit you, and he speaks to animals, Maggie. Hit. Speak. Animals. Bad. Maggie ground the heels of her palms into her temples. *That's right. Gather your wits, Margaret O'Hare. It doesn't matter who or what he is; the man made it clear he intends to keep you prisoner and have his way with you. You. Need. To. Leave.*

Doggone it! All right. Play nice, get his guard down, and make a break for it.

This was her only choice. After all, her father wouldn't notice her missing and the people in the village minded their own business when it came to outsiders, so no one would come looking for her. She was on her own. And strangely, she didn't feel afraid; she felt like this entire situation was some bizarre test of her will.

Chaam huffed and then proceeded to grind his teeth, never breaking his feral gaze. "I am very sorry I slapped you. A rather large thirsty mosquito landed on your face. I sometimes forget my own strength."

Oh sure! And I'm Al Capone's private Alcatraz chef.

Maggie, play nice. Find something pleasant to talk about.

"I forgive you." Maggie pasted on a sugary sweet smile. "Say, what's that cologne you're wearing? It smells divine."

Suspicion flickered in his glorious turquoise eyes. "It is my natural scent. It is infused with potent male pheromones to induce euphoria. Like brain candy."

Eww. "Brain candy? I'm not so sure that candy made from brains would induce euphoria."

A smile twitched across his lips. "My apologies. That is a term often used by my sister. She is quite mad, but her odd phrases have a way of sticking. What I meant to say was that my scent is a treat to the senses." *Treat to the senses? Carrying around that huge ego must give him back pain. And is he referring to the same sister who sprang from the lake?* She was about to ask but had a feeling the topic would only drag out the conversation.

"So, you say you're a deity of some sort. Got any superpowers besides that *brain candy* of yours?"

He stood a little taller. "In fact, yes. But we can discuss the details later." He gestured toward a small circle of stones toward the edge of the clearing farthest from the lake. A large log lay beside the fire ring. "Please sit. I've brought you wine and food to eat while I build a fire and set up our hammock."

Our *hammock?*

Chaam reached into the satchel she'd noticed him carrying and handed her a small bundle wrapped in paper and string. It smelled heavenly.

She sat on the log and unraveled the package. Fresh handmade tortillas, a wedge of hard cheese, and a few Mexican pastries—her favorite, deep-fried dough sprinkled with sugar and cinnamon.

"Ummm, churros. How did you know?" Maggie's stomach growled like a...

Like a... Chaam?

She took a bite, then another and another. Before she knew it, she'd devoured every last crumb.

"You were hungry, I see," Chaam said in a shocked sort of way.

Yes. She'd finished it all. Without sharing. Take that! "Oh my. Was that intended for both of us?"

Chaam kneeled and ignited the flames. "Yes, but don't worry; I do not *need* to eat."

"Right. Because you're a god."

He laughed. "You still do not believe me."

Well, now that they were on the subject...

Hold on! Play nice.

"Sure I do," she said.

"Good. Then you know it is unwise to anger me." Crouched, he glanced over his shoulder and winked. "Now, I want you to tell me who and what you really are."

Tread carefully, Margaret. Very carefully.

"What do you think I am?" she asked.

He turned away and poked at the flames with a stick. "Something other than human."

"Why would you think that?" Did he know something she didn't?

"My kind cannot have intimate contact—or much contact in any form—with mortals. Our energy is deadly."

"So because you kissed me, and I didn't keel over…?"

He nodded yes and then sat beside her. Close. Too close. Her body began to tingle with that familiar tension.

Oh no. Not again. She scooted down the log, but it wasn't nearly far enough. A couple of continents might do the trick. An entire solar system would be better.

He ignored the move, pulled a bottle of wine from his satchel, and poured the ruby liquid into two metal cups, one of which he offered to her. "Come closer. I do not bite."

"But you hit, bully, and kidnap. Biting would really make the package complete." She slapped her hand over her mouth.

He rubbed his forehead. "You are correct, Maggie. I haven't treated you kindly, and it's no way to start our life—excuse me—our *evening* together."

Life? Crap! He really, *really* didn't plan to let her go. Ever.

"But I promise," he said, "to spend the entire

night making it up to you." Once again he held up the wine.

The entire night? He's out of his loco sombrero if he thinks I'm sleeping with him!

For the briefest of moments, Maggie considered telling Chaam the truth: Her father was missing and she needed to go. This insane little game had to end. But what if he said no? And if he knew her situation, he'd deduce her desperation to leave. He'd never let his guard down. No, she'd keep the facts of her father to herself and stay the course. Play nice. Guard down. Run like hell.

She pasted back the smile, moved down the log, and took the cup. "Why don't we get to know each other a little better?" She sipped the sweet, tangy wine. "You were saying something about not being able to touch humans?"

He made an approving nod and continued, "I can suppress my energy if I focus my thoughts on doing so. But when being intimate, such pleasure does not create an atmosphere where one is in control. A lesson learned the hard—"

He stopped.

"Did you hurt someone?"

His gaze dropped to the fire. "No. Another of my kind attempted to take a lover, many times, in fact. Each instance ended poorly."

"Poorly? As in *dead* poorly?"

"Worse. Her lack of success has driven her mad. But let us not discuss this. Our situation is special.

You are special." He looked at her with those divine eyes, and an intense wordless exchange ignited.

I want you, his eyes said.

Do you, now?

Oh yes. With every pulse of my immortal light.

You don't even know me.

I know your soul; that's all I need.

This is insanity.

Welcome to my world.

Your world scares me.

Maggie retreated and threw back the rest of her wine. The liquid brought a welcome warmth to her chest despite the constant tropical breeze skating off the calm lake behind her. Every second she spent in his presence brought her closer to a cold reality lurking just beneath the surface: Part of her wanted to believe the crazy things he told her. Part of her wanted him.

This is *insanity. I need to leave.*

She moved her feet in front of the crackling fire and gave her toes a wiggle. How far would she get without shoes when she made a run for it? Solid blackness had replaced the lush greens of the jungle, and night had set in.

You have to try for your father.

"So you believe I'm special because you can touch me?" she said.

"And because of the vision."

"Vision?" Obviously, she'd seen it, too, when they kissed; however, she didn't know what to make of it. Nor did she want to discuss it. She just wanted to leave.

"Do not deny you saw it," he said.

"I saw no such thing."

He laughed.

"Are you doubting me?" she asked.

He nodded, and his long black hair fell over his face. "Yes. In fact, I am. Perhaps it is time to disclose that among my many powers, I know when humans lie."

"Aha, see! You know when *humans* lie. I must be human." *I can't believe I'm making this argument.*

He frowned and pushed back his hair. "Not likely."

"To my knowledge, my parents are human. Well, my mother was. God rest her sweet soul."

Chaam's frown softened into something resembling compassion. "I am sorry to hear you lost your mother. Were you young?"

"No. It happened about six months ago. A heart attack while at work."

Wow. Maggie hadn't ever said that out loud. It felt good talking about it. And it felt surprisingly good talking to Chaam. Come to think of it, this was the first time in months that she'd felt so at ease. The realization added one more layer of complexity to the situation.

"She was a movie actress," she continued, staring at the flames, avoiding direct eye contact. "A really good one, but her real passion was teaching children at the local dance academy."

"It sounds like she was a beautiful person," he said.

Maggie nodded. "The most beautiful person I've ever known. I think it's the reason my father wanted to come here, to escape her memory."

Her father. God, how he'd changed. The man she used to know had never run from anything. He embraced life, as did her mother. Together, the two were like perpetual motion. Unstoppable. And wildly in love until the very end. Maggie could only hope to find something so epic. She'd dreamed of it, but sadly, all she'd found were men who left her frigid in the feelings department. And when she said frigid, she meant deep freeze, like she was some horrible woman-shaped iceberg with fashion sense. And quite a bit of baggage. Stylish baggage, of course.

It's not that way with Chaam, now is it?

Damn it. No, it isn't. Maybe that was why her mind kept spinning in the mud. Dirty, dirty, sexy mud she wanted to roll in with Chaam.

"It's why I had to fight to come on this trip," she added, still refusing to look into his eyes, knowing she would like—no, love—what she saw.

"You remind him of her, don't you?"

She felt his eyes burning on her. "Yes."

He placed his hand on her cheek. "Look at me, Margaret. Don't be afraid."

Could she dare to meet his gaze?

Maggie slowly turned her head. When she did, the larger-than-life man sitting before her seemed to have reached a heightened level of exquisiteness. She drank in the well-defined angles of his cheekbones and jaw, the perfect, yet large proportions of his muscles and limbs. She marveled at his flawless golden brown skin glowing with the oranges and yellows of the flickering firelight. Then there were his eyes. Two hypnotic jewels of seduction that drew her in like sexual gravity, urging her to leap across that wide-open stretch of insanity and take him up on that offer of carnal pleasures.

With exaggerated caution, Chaam reached out and brushed her cheek. She leaned into his hand and basked in its warmth. "If you look like she did," he said, "I can understand why your father is unable to recover from his loss. You are divine, Margaret O'Hare. The gods themselves could not compete with your perfection." He leaned in to kiss her.

Horsefeathers! Maggie popped up. What was she thinking? She'd become completely engrossed in this conversation. "I need to use the powder room."

Chaam tilted his head to one side. "Powder room?"

"I have to, you know, listen to the call of nature?"

Chaam looked from side to side. "You hear them, too? How very odd. Perhaps it is a side effect."

What? Heavens no. She wasn't crazy. "Uh, I

have to empty my bladder."

"Oh. Of course." He gestured toward the jungle. "You may use any tree you like."

This was her chance. She headed straight for the dark jungle.

"Any tree where I can see you," he added.

Drat! She stopped and found herself staring straight up a wall of solid, unnerving man. How had he moved so fast? "You, you can't honestly th-think-think that a lady would allow a man to watch her."

"I am not a man. I am a god, and there is little I haven't seen except for these rooms made from powder you speak of. How do the walls stay up?"

Ugh! Impossible, crazy, gorgeous man. "Magic. I can explain later, but right now, I need privacy." She smiled as sweet as apple pie with ice cream on top. "Please?"

Chaam considered her request for a moment. "If you are not back in one minute, I will send the jaguar after you. You cannot hide from that nose, and he is all too desperate to do anything to please me. He has his eye on a very fine female he's been unable to woo."

Woo? Now the animals were *wooing* each other? Oh boy. He really was insane.

"I understand." She scurried off into the brush, praying those crazed animals were not waiting in the shadows like he'd said.

Maggie, are you forgetting? They stared at you for three hours like furry sentinels.

Damn it, Maggie. You need to run. Now.

So she did.

Twenty Minutes Later

"I told you not to run." Chaam wrapped her twisted ankle in strips of linen he'd made from tearing apart his shirt.

Maggie huffed, crossed her arms over her chest, and lay back in the hammock strung between two large trees near the campfire. "Well, what the deviled-ham sandwich did you expect? You hold me prisoner, tell me you're going to rob me of my innocence—"

Hunched over her ankle, Chaam bucked. "I never. Ever. Said I would force you."

"But you—"

"Woman, I merely stated the facts, and I will gladly state them again. I plan to be inside you tonight." He leaned over her face, his breath hot and sweet in her nostrils, filling her with every erotic thought known to womankind. "But you will beg me for it," he whispered.

She clamped her eyes shut. "Wh-why do you say those things?"

He brushed his fingertips over her lips. "I always speak the truth without shame or remorse. And with time, you will learn to do the same. Meanwhile, do you need to be reminded of the vision?"

She shook her head no.

"I think you do. I think you need to see our naked, sweat-slicked bodies twisting together like two hungry serpents, to see my hands gripping your hips as you straddle my cock."

Maggie's eyes flew open. How could he say such vulgar things? "I assure you I did not dream that. You're a despicable monster."

Chaam straightened his back, made a little bow, and gestured gallantly toward the jungle. "Very well. If this is your opinion, then you may go."

Was this a trick? "What do you mean?"

"I'll let you go."

"Just like that?"

He nodded. "In exchange for a kiss."

"Huh?"

He *tsk*ed at her. "Do not play stupid. That is my price. A kiss. Prove that you did not feel what I feel, that you did not see what I saw, and I will let you go."

Oh hell! But she had seen it. She had! *Ugh.* This situation was insane. *Think. Think. Think.* She'd already kissed him once and survived with her wit and virtue intact. Yes, she could handle another.

"Fine. I'll kiss you, then you'll let me go," she replied.

He yanked her from the hammock and held her so tightly that her toes dangled in the air. The sensation of their bodies pressed together—that warm, smooth, bare chest pressed against her palms—was intolerable. Tension, tension, so much delicious tension. Oh gods, she was about to sail that ship again.

This man didn't fight fair.

She shot him a scowl. *Oh! And he knows it!* Every inch of that wickedly gorgeous face had male smugness written all over it.

"W-well," she said, "what are you waiting for? Kiss me."

He plunged to take his prize.

Chapter Four

This was not just a kiss. No. He would open himself to her, and she would know his torment, know the slow-burn ache of his loneliness. She would know his heart, soul, and mind. And then they would make love and uncover the bittersweet truth.

What would he do if she was his mate? Did it matter? Any way he looked at it, the situation was impossible. His world did not fit neatly with a mortal's, and he could never turn his back on what he was. Yet he couldn't stop himself from wanting to move forward, from wanting to discover why fate had pulled them together. His lips slammed against Maggie's, and his tongue thrust inside her mouth. Into her, he poured every raw ounce of unsated sexual hunger he'd endured. No more games.

Several hellacious moments slid by before her walls of superficial, manmade decency and righteousness crumbled. She threw her arms around his neck and kissed him back. Hard. Needy. Uninhibited.

Yes…

His entire body instantly flooded with her light, which reached every corner of his soul. *Holy hell, man. She has to be your mate.* He did not need to make love to her to sense the powerful bond between them. But instead of it seeming like an insufferable fate, as he'd imagined it would, the connection filled him with quiet strength and a profound peace of mind. No matter what came next, he would find a way to be with her.

"Say you want me," he panted between kisses.

Maggie peeled herself away and looked him in the eyes. "What *are* you?"

"Does it really matter, Margaret? You feel we are meant to be together, and I have waited my entire existence for you. You feel the truth, so say it. Say you want me."

What could she say? Whatever he was, he'd just blown her ship deep into the swelling waves of uncharted waters. And that kiss! It was an ancient cyclone of nomadic wind that had journeyed across thousands of centuries, witnessing his life. Every exhilarating emotion and mundane thought, every beat of his neglected heart—she watched it all. She saw the faces of everyone he'd helped, his brethren, his foes. She felt his frustration for the role thrust upon him and the compulsion that kept him going even when he believed he might go mad if he lived another day as a god.

Oh lord! Her mind sputtered. It was as though she'd been living on a Wild West movie set and had suddenly decided to peer through the saloon window, only to find the real world just on the other side.

He was telling the truth. But how could gods exist without anyone knowing? The world was not at all what she'd believed.

A lifetime of manufactured façades crumbled at her feet, and in this new reality, each sliver of bone in her trembling body sang with the truth: She was born to be with him. This was why no other man had ever touched her heart. *I'm not broken…*

Maggie sighed. Yes, she wanted him. She would never breathe again without him. She would shrivel up and die this very instant without the rough touch of his hands on her bare skin, without knowing his lips intimately exploring her body, and without having him deep inside her. Every cell in Maggie's body threatened to collapse if her body didn't get its way.

"Yes," she finally purred.

A twinge of wicked victory shaped his full, stubble-framed lips. "Yes, what?"

"You're really going to make me say it?"

"Naturally."

"I want you," she said with her mouth, but her eyes boldly told him what was now in her heart and soul: the insane, magnanimous, epic truth that words could never articulate: She was his. At least, she sure as hell wanted to be.

"That wasn't begging."

"Don't push it," she hissed.

"I didn't say you have to beg with words."

He gently set her on the ground, steadying her on her good ankle. "Show me how you feel with your body." He undid the top button of her dress.

Her insides twisted into a knot of anticipation.

Another button.

And another.

She swallowed.

"Lovely." He ran his callused fingertips over the swells of her half-exposed breasts, and strummed those taut ropes, which braced her sails, like the strings of a guitar.

His hand stopped. "And what is this?"

It was a necklace. She hadn't removed it since the day her father—*Christ!* Her father!

She stepped back and fisted shut the open panels of her dress. "There's something I have to tell you." She instinctively knew there could be no secrets between them.

Oh God. I've gone insane, haven't I? I can't believe this is all happening.

Chaam closed the gap between them. "Can it wait? If it's about the species question, I assure you I do not care. I would still want you even if you were part chupacabra."

What the flapjack is a chupacabra?

She shook her head no. "My father is missing. That's why I was in the jungle. And as much as I want to do this with you—as incredibly insane as that is—which I won't argue with because you are clearly, clearly something different, and I am clearly,

clearly not ever going to get you out of my system or head or life because I *did* see the vision, and it was...*wow*...and now I've gone all goofy for you—but I have to find him."

"Goofy? I assume this means you desire me?"

She nodded.

"Is the desire deep and consuming?"

She nodded again.

Chaam gloated with a smirk, just a little. "How long has he been missing?"

"Three days. And he hasn't been well."

"I assume you're referring to his mental state?"

She nodded.

"Am I in time for s'mores?"

Chaam shoved Maggie behind him and then groaned with relief. "For fuck's sake, Cimil, how many times have I told you not to sneak up on me?"

"Five thousand, two hundred, and twenty-two," Cimil said. "Only six thousand, three hundred and fifty more times to go before I listen!"

Maggie immediately recognized the strange redhead, only now she wore a mariachi outfit, complete with dazzling sombrero. A loco-sombrero, of course.

"Funny. Mind telling me what the hell you're doing here?" Chaam asked.

"What? Can't a goddess of the underworld go for a leisurely stroll in the jungle for a little fresh air without having any hidden agendas, especially ones having to do with mischief, mayhem, and world domination?"

"No," Chaam replied.

Maggie felt strangely relieved that Chaam didn't seem particularly fond of the bizarre woman, because she sure as hell scared the crap out of Maggie.

"She said she was looking for you when I saw her earlier," Maggie whispered over Chaam's shoulder.

Chaam glanced at Maggie. "You already met my sister?"

Maggie nodded, but actually wanted to wince or make some sort of sour face to express her complete distaste of this woman he called his sister. "Uh-huh. She came out of the lake when I was stuck on the dock."

Chaam whispered, "What did she say?"

"Only the truth, brother," Cimil spouted. "Maggie is your destiny."

Chaam growled. "You're up to something. I know it." He pointed toward the dock. "You. There. Now."

Cimil rolled her eyes and then began marching. "Gods. They're so bossy," she whispered as she passed Maggie.

"No, he's perfect," Maggie hissed. Surprisingly, she didn't appreciate anyone bad-mouthing Chaam.

"Oh, you just wait," Cimil replied and trailed behind her brother to the dock.

While Maggie buttoned her dress, Chaam and his sister had an intense conversation. Not that

Maggie could see their faces in the dark, but the water did a nice job of carrying their voices. Maggie had never heard the f-word so many times. She'd need to talk to Chaam about his abrasive, ungentlemanly vocabulary later. For the time being, however, she listened intently as Cimil swore over and over again that she hadn't come to collect any—*shit!* Had she said "souls"?

"You fucking expect me to believe you're here for fun?" Chaam asked Cimil.

"Yes! I heard about that cricket, and well, I...dammit, Chaam! You know what happened with Alberto. I completely overreacted. I've been searching for him ever since."

"That should teach you not to turn humans into insects. And that should *really* teach you not to set them free in the jungle!"

Oh, my lord, Maggie thought. *They can't be serious.*

"I didn't mean to hurt him," Cimil said. "I merely wanted to teach him a lesson for spending all his time with that little slut!"

"Cimil! She was his sister. She was his *sick* sister! Have you no compassion?"

Long pause. "Is this a trick question?" Cimil asked.

"Never mind," he replied. "I am calling in that favor you owe me."

"Now?" she whined.

"Yes." Chaam's voice softened to a whisper too

low for Maggie to hear.

After several moments, the two returned to the fire. "Maggie, Cimil has kindly agreed to look for your father, so if you could—"

"What? You're sending *her*?" Maggie asked.

Cimil hissed. "Watch it, cupcake. I may look crazy, but I'm actually...actually, yeah. I'm crazy. I mean, you have no idea." She snorted.

Maggie suddenly realized that Cimil must've been the one Chaam had spoken of earlier; the god who'd tried to take lovers and lost her mind.

Chaam pulled Maggie to the side. "Leaving you here alone is not an option; there are many dangers in this jungle. So either she goes or I go."

Maggie certainly didn't want to stay alone with crazy-hat over there. "I see."

Chaam cupped her face. His hands were warm and rough, and as inappropriate as it was given the situation, Maggie couldn't help but notice that sweet tension coiling right on cue.

He threaded one hand through her hair and kissed her quickly. "I knew you would see it my way. Besides, you and I have some unfinished begging to attend to."

After Maggie gave her father's description and the approximate location of the excavation site, Chaam spent a full ten minutes describing Cimil's fate in explicit detail right down to her crazy cuticles if she didn't find Maggie's father pronto.

Ironically, the graphic threat didn't sour Maggie's impression of Chaam; it cemented the truth in her bones. He was a deity. How had she not seen it? The power and authority he yielded leaked from every word, every gesture. Even Cimil's blasé response—eye rolling and foot stomping, but never showing fear—indicated she was not of this world. Or maybe that was a sign of her bat-shit craziness? Who knew?

Chaam watched Cimil's silhouette fade into the night and then threw two logs on the waning campfire. "Are you ready?"

"Ready?" Maggie asked.

He dipped his head. "Yes. *Ready.*"

Maggie's entire body solidified into a mass of tense muscles. "You mean…"

He made no production of reaching for the buttons of her dress.

"Wait!" She gripped his hand. "I want to know something."

"Yes?" His eyes flickered with impatience.

"You said that you'd waited for me your entire existence?"

He nodded and a warm glowing smile stretched across his lips. And yes, she pathetically melted inside.

"Are you absolutely sure it's me?" she blurted.

He nodded again. "I think I knew from the moment I touched you. Fate brought us together. I feel it."

She felt it too now. At least, that was what she

thought she felt. It was so dang difficult to believe. "But what if you're mistaken?"

"I am never wrong about such things."

"I'll need a little more than that if I'm going to give myself to you."

He didn't bother to contemplate a response. "I have spent thousands upon thousands of years assisting mortals bond with their true loves. I have become very adept at recognizing the signs of two souls meant for one another."

"But didn't you say you're the God of Male..." *Oh, what was it? Whoopee? Friskiness? Horniness.*

"Virility," he said.

"Yes, that. Which means you help men..."

"Have sex. But I do not waste my time with those who simply want to fuck. Although, fucking," he slid his finger over the curve of her jaw, "certainly has its place and purpose."

To hear him say *that* word in *that* way spiked her mind with vivid sexual images. Images that sent her heart on a thumping rampage. God, she actually wanted him to say it again.

"I help males," he continued, "who have found their true love but have lost their way and are unable to take that next, all-important step. Sometimes it is fear of rejection or fear they will not please the woman, especially if it is his first time."

"But why do you only help men?" she said.

He gave her a "you-must-be-joking" look.

"What? It's a legitimate question."

"Because," he replied, "men are idiots."

Can't argue there.

"More precisely, they are idiots when it comes to intimacy. Women have a natural gift for such things."

Again. Can't argue there.

"What do you do to help them?" she asked.

He shrugged like a man who had all the answers. "Depends on the situation. Sometimes, it's merely a question of removing the negative energy they've accumulated—fear is like a cancer of the spirit. Other times, I must compel them to simply push ahead, so to speak. And then there are those occasions when I must teach them precisely what to do."

She swallowed. "Teach them? You-you mean actually show them how to…?"

He reached for her hand and kissed the inside of her wrist. The roughness of his whiskers and the soft warmth of his lips speared right through her central nervous system.

"Oh yes," he whispered. "I show them how to please a woman, specifically, their woman. Every female is different."

Her insides clenched. "You-you know what *every* woman wants?"

He stepped in and pressed his tall, powerful frame against her. "Yes. It is a gift." He leaned in slowly and placed his lips to her ear. "I merely look at a female, and I know." He brushed his lips down the length of her neck.

"Wha-wha-what is it that I wa-wa-want?" *Brain? Are you there? Please don't abandon me now.*

His hot breath tickled the curve of her neck.

Oooh. Yes. She wanted that. How did he know?

He placed a soft, sucking kiss over the same spot and then pulled her against the hardness between his legs.

Yesss. That too. Horsefeathers...he's good.

He then slanted his hot lips possessively over hers, slid his tongue past her teeth, and rhythmically stroked her mouth in time with the rocking of his hips.

Suddenly, a wild and uninhibited Margaret she never knew existed took over. This Margaret didn't care about propriety or anything rational. This Margaret panted and clawed and wanted him deeper. This Margaret returned each thrust of his tongue with one of her own and desired only to devour every male inch of his large, insanely hard body.

With a frantic flurry of hands and kisses, Chaam stripped away her dress and undergarments and backed her into the finely woven hammock. She raised her hand to pull him down with her, but he moved back and drilled her with his turquoise gaze, willing her to stay put.

Chaam leisurely slid off his white cotton trousers and straightened to his full height. Shoulders broad and straight, he proudly displayed each unbreakable ripple of his abdomen, the swells of his chest, and the sexy, unmistakably masculine patch of black hair surrounding the one object she'd crudely obsessed over since she'd first spotted him toweling off. She'd not seen his manhood then, but now she stared right at the thing. It jutted into the air like a thick saber made of solid flesh.

She squirmed just a little as the heat between her legs made it abundantly clear that his large, pulsing erection was exactly what she needed to ease the aching tension deep inside.

Are you kidding? Look at the size of that thing. Do you really think it's going to feel pleasant?

Wild Margaret went running for the hills.

"What's the matter?" He glanced over one shoulder and then the other. "Is that damned jaguar back?"

"No, it's…well, I've never…" She scrutinized her body, then his daunting erection.

"Oh. I see." He relaxed with a cocky smile. "Not to worry, hammocks have been around for thousands of years. I assure you it is very secure. And," he paused, "I know what I'm doing."

"No. I meant your size is so…" *Drat. How should I say it?* "You're large, all right? Really damned large, and I—"

"I am told this hammock," he interrupted, "can hold the weight of ten men, not that I wish to see that. Besides," he leaned over for a kiss, hovering just above her lips, "I know what I'm doing. I am the God of Male Virility. I practically invented sex."

Oh, potato salad! "I've never been with a man," she blurted.

A radiant smile, one that displayed almost every pearly white in his gorgeous mouth, leapt across his face. "Neither have I."

"Amusing."

Seriousness took over and his eyes locked on hers. "I have never been with anyone, either."

"A virgin? You?"

"Yes," he replied without the faintest hint of embarrassment.

The thought had never occurred to her, but given what she now knew—gulp, gods were real?—about his kind, well, of course he was a virgin.

He then lifted his eyebrows in such a way that said, "And I know you want some," however, his mouth said, "And I assure you, I know exactly what I'm doing. I know exactly what you want."

Without breaking his gaze, he lay over her, smoothly placing himself between her legs. This simple act of his delicious, warm body pressing intimately against hers was the most sensual thing she'd ever experienced. And the moment his lips touched hers, the moment his rough hand cupped her breast, the moment the tip of his stiff cock prodded her sensitive opening, she understood what it meant to beg with her body.

Combustion!

She slid her arms around the sides of his tight,

narrow hips and cupped his solid, smooth backside, the one she'd already decided deserved a shrine (or maybe two? or five?) to urge him closer.

With his strength and sizeable mass, he easily resisted her invitation to plunge inside. "No," he whispered with a hot breath in her ear, "it will hurt less if I work it in slowly. You will enjoy it much more."

But didn't he say he knew what she wanted? Because if he did, he'd know she was shamelessly begging for every hard inch.

She pulled his mouth to hers, slid her tongue past those sweet delicious lips, and again raised her hips toward the head of his cock, driving him just a nudge deeper.

His eyes clamped shut and he groaned.

"You weren't listening very well, because this is what I want," she whispered.

His eyes flew open, and something animalistic and greedy flickered inside those orbs of deep turquoise.

Before she could mutter another word, he leaned into her. She cried out as he slid deep inside.

Although she'd begged him for it, he knew her pain had been sharp. He'd witnessed countless females taken for the first time. Generally he watched from his realm and provided help to the clumsy males who were on course to spill themselves before getting past the threshold, but no amount of spectating could have prepared him for the ecstasy of taking Margaret O'Hare. Being deep inside her tight, slick heat, merging their bodies together, made him feel alive with sinful rapture.

"Are you all right?" He fought the urge to begin rocking himself deeper, knowing her body was processing the raw, conflicting sensations of pain and pleasure.

Eyes shut tight, she nodded.

He brushed her swollen lips with his and released a tiny pulse of his light to help her heal quickly. "Tell me when you want more," he whispered.

Within moments her heated mouth returned to his. She pulled back her hips and pushed into him.

A groan involuntarily escaped his mouth. He'd never imagined...

The sensual tension immediately began to build with each delicious stroke of friction. Her fingernails dug into his back as she pulled him deeper, working him in and out in a steady rhythm. And just when he believed his pleasure could not escalate another titillating inch, it did. She screamed his name into the night, her body going rigid with her release while her inner muscles contracted, milking him.

He felt the hot liquid burst from his cock, and with it, her name poured from his lips.

No, he would never let this woman go.

Chapter Five

"Have there always been this many stars? And have they always been this bright?" Maggie gazed in wonderment at the cloudless night sky over Chaam's shoulder while he showered her neck, ear, and shoulder with kisses. She'd never felt so complete, so content, so happy.

"Thank you for this, Maggie. My precious Maggie," he whispered repeatedly.

He's thanking me? Never in her wildest dreams could she have imagined this day, this man, the insanity of the situation. So damned right. Every second of it. She should be thanking him.

She sighed. "I feel like I'm seeing the world for the very first time."

"And what do you see?" he asked.

Euphoria, love, peace in my heart... "You." The instant he'd entered her, he was all she saw.

One moment she had been an omnipresent light hovering over the world, watching thousands of people. Nowhere. Everywhere. All at once. She felt their desperation, their desolate hearts, their prayers for help. Who knew so much silent suffering filled the world? It saddened her deeply because she'd been one of them. But for some, Maggie included, there was a light. There was hope. Chaam.

And he was right. His gift wasn't paving a man's way to sex, but for the union of two souls who were meant to be together but somehow got lost along the way. There had been so many he had helped, millions upon millions, yet Chaam never once spurned them because they'd found something he longed for. Instead, his hope—that his day, too, might come—only grew.

Maggie's heart filled with unspeakable pride, knowing such devotion and faith drove the person she'd given herself to.

Then she witnessed him charging through the jungle. Through his ears, she heard his heavy breaths. Through his eyes, she saw the brilliant emerald greens of the trees and the perfection of the pristine blue sky. Through his heart, she felt his emptiness, his need for true companionship. So much sorrow—she could relate. But the moment Chaam had moved inside her, she knew it was more than a carnal lust being satisfied; they were two souls finding a missing piece. They'd finally have a chance to break free from their heavy pasts because together, they were strong. Together, they could make their own fate. Together, they were in control.

Yes, she saw everything so clearly now. So, so clearly.

Life was nothing but a constant flow, the universe breathing in and out. *I am part of it.* Every mundane action, every thought, every smile or frown shown even to a stranger created a chain of events, like ripples in a pond.

Fear had once blinded her, but now she knew: She mattered. She mattered. She mattered. Just like Chaam, everything she did mattered. And it filled her with power and purpose.

"You see me?" He nudged the pendant of her necklace to one side and placed a gentle kiss on the hollow of her neck. "Who am I?"

"You're magic. My magic." She stroked the back of his head. His long hair was soft and magnificent. She could spend an eternity petting it *and everything else*.

Chaam lifted his head. "Magic?" He beamed. "Well, that is quite the compliment. I've been called many things, but a magician…"

Still inside her, he gently pushed his hips forward. His erection had not shown the slightest signs of flagging.

A sharp wave of ecstasy bolted through her, and she gasped. "Oh yes. Magic."

Slowly, he rocked his hips. "Let me show you my next trick. I think I know exactly what you want."

Several hours later, Maggie's deliciously sore body was a heap of weak, quivering muscles. Who knew hammocks were so versatile? Sideways, diagonally, on the top or on the bottom, the netting molded to their forms and allowed the night breeze to cool their heated, sweat-covered bodies.

I will never sleep in a bed again.

Chaam extracted himself carefully from the hammock, and the campfire, now a murmuring pile of glowing embers, afforded her a glimpse of his glorious backside. Smooth, round, firm. Even the rippling muscles in his back were something to behold. The first chance she got, she would put paint to canvas and capture every inch of him. Those gorgeous toes included. Someone needed to pay the appropriate homage to this specimen of male perfection.

"Where are you going?" she asked.

He leaned down and scooped her into his arms. "*We* are going for a swim. It will revive you."

Revive her? Dear sweet God of Male Virility, he wanted more?

The lake was considerably warmer than the air outside. Like tepid bathwater, really. The two splashed and played and Chaam found himself not wanting to go very long without touching that creamy, soft skin, the feminine curve of her hips, or those perfectly round breasts. And those lips? Two plump little pillows meant for seduction. But of all her sinful gifts, he loved her eyes most. The darkest of browns, almost black. They were wide and bright and the most glorious windows to her glorious soul—a soul of the purest color he'd ever seen.

Making love to her had been the most amazing experience of his existence. He didn't know if he felt love or if the gods were capable of such feelings, but attempting to define such emotions with a word would not do. She'd embedded her light inside his soul.

Waist high in the water, he pulled Maggie into his arms. She shivered.

"Cold?" he asked.

"Can you warm me up?"

With the darkness of night, he could not see her face, but he knew she grinned.

"I can figure something out." He picked her up and threw her over his shoulder.

She laughed and squirmed. "Put me down!"

He smacked her fleshy backside. "Silence, woman." He easily climbed from the water and deposited her on the dock.

"Woman? I'm a lady."

"Not anymore."

"What!" She giggled and slapped his bare chest. "Well, whose fault is that?"

"Mine. All mine," he said. But was she? His, that is? Saints, he'd not thought the situation through. Christ. Maggie had never answered his question. What was she? If not immortal, she would eventually die and leave him.

Leave. Him.

He gripped her firmly by the shoulders. "Maggie, you will tell me what you are. No more games."

She squirmed. "You're hurting me. What's gotten into you?"

He released her and hissed, "I'm sorry. I often forget my strength. But dammit, woman! Tell me."

"I told you, I'm human." The darkness masked her expression, but fear permeated her voice.

"Impossible!"

"Why? Why won't you believe me?" she argued.

"Because gods cannot make love to humans."

"But I am human! I am. Can't you look into my eyes or something? I'm not lying." She tugged him toward the fire. "Put another log on so you can look."

"Gods dammit." He stood firm and ran his hand over his dripping wet hair.

Maggie rubbed his arm. "What is it? Tell me."

Fear. It welled inside him.

For fuck's sake. He'd never felt this emotion before. But then again, he'd never had anything to lose.

"If you are telling the truth, Maggie, then you will die someday."

"Oh," was all she replied.

He couldn't lose her. Not now.

"Maggie, you will come to my world. We will ask the gods to grant you immortality."

Immortality?

"I'm...I'm sorry. But did you just say immortality?"

"Yes," he said.

She could not see his face, but she felt the stark pain in his voice. He was serious. "Is it really possible?"

"Yes."

Live forever? With him? God save her—*or is that* gods?—she had no idea what to do or say. What would be the repercussion? Did he even love her? She hoped with all her heart that he did because after everything she'd seen and felt, she knew there had been a reason no other man had ever reached her heart; it belonged to Chaam, and it always would.

"Why? Tell me why," she said.

"Maggie, I have waited my entire existence for you. The universe has given me this gift. You are mine, my reward for thousands of years of dedication and loyalty. I'm not about to let you go."

That was not what she'd hoped to hear. In fact, he made her sound like a booby prize. Not the naughty kind, but the silly kind.

"Maggie, I will not take no for an answer."

"What will happen to my soul?"

"Your soul? I-I do not know. I suppose it stays with you."

"You're a god, but you don't know?"

"We don't know everything, Maggie. We simply know more."

She needed time to think. It was all too much to take in. And now she knew the truth: there were no decisions, no actions without consequence. Everything mattered.

"Can I have some time?" she asked.

Anger radiated from his body. "You may have until sunrise."

"Why are you pushing me, Chaam?"

"If you speak the truth, then you are mortal. Mortals die by the thousands every second. I'm not about to risk anything happening to the one person I cannot live without."

A tiny fissure opened in her heart as she thought of him suffering for an eternity. Maybe he didn't love her. She didn't know. But he needed her, and she loved him.

Yes. The situation was pure insanity. One big loco-sombrero.

She'd met a man in the jungle today who wasn't really a man. She became his prisoner, then his lover. Now she loved him.

Insanity.

And it didn't matter if he loved her back; she would give her loco-sombrero to ensure he never suffered again.

"What if the other gods say no?" she asked.

Her backhanded acceptance sparked a glorious smile on her god's face. "They will not. Asking permission is customary—an offering to their egos. Once those are satisfied, they will not stand in our way."

"Are they like you?"

He laughed. "Yes and no. We are all unique, although my brothers Votan and Zac are physically similar to me when in their human forms, so I will warn you now not to get any ideas."

As if she could ever look at another man—errr—deity.

"I want you. Just you," she said.

Chaam kissed her, and his joy washed over her like a burst of warm sunshine.

"And you shall have me," he said.

"Will I?" She slid her hands around his waist and leaned in. She couldn't get enough of him or his wickedly sweet smell. And now that she'd accepted who he was, what he was, his grandness felt magnified somehow. Maybe because she understood all that he'd done, all that he'd sacrificed for humanity.

But did he know the world was an infinitely better place because he was part of it? The first chance she had, she would tell him.

But for the time being…

Chaam laid her down on the dock and hovered over her. His silhouette against the night sky was awe inspiring. With his mouth he sought for her neck and swept her hair to one side. As he did, the necklace she wore became tangled in her wet mane and pulled uncomfortably on a few strands at her nape. She gave the chain a little tug and it broke free, but not before ripping a clump of hair out with it.

She screamed as scorching, searing pain ripped through her. She fell to the side, writhing in agony. Had her body been torn into two?

"Maggie!" She heard Chaam screaming in some

dark corner of her mind. “Maggie, speak to me!”

She couldn’t breathe. She couldn’t move. She was going to die this very moment, and now he would suffer for eternity.

Blackness.

Chapter Six

November 2, 1934 (Day of the Dead)

Chaam stared at Maggie's immobile body stretched across the dock. *What the hell just happened?*

He dropped to his knees and placed his ear over her heart. The organ thrummed for two blissful seconds and then produced a choppy monstrosity of sound reminiscent of a cat walking across the keys of a piano.

He jerked his head up and then lowered it again, hovering just above her chest. The heartbeat returned to normal.

He repeated the act of touching her and breaking contact twice more. Each time produced the same result. Until he placed the necklace over her stomach.

Christ, no. This cannot be.

Maggie began to stir. "Chaam?" she asked with a bleary voice.

He resisted having a very unmanly display of hysterics. "Thank the gods, you're all right."

She sat up and rubbed her red eyes. It was nearly dawn now, the sky a brilliant pallet of pinks and lavenders. "What happened?"

His relief and shock shifted to wrath. "This happened." He held up the tiny teardrop-shaped black stone mounted on a smooth silver plaque.

She reached for the vacant spot on her neck.

"Where did you get this?" he demanded.

"Why are you angry?"

He crouched and touched her arm.

"Ouch!" She jerked away.

"Who are you?" he demanded.

"But I don't understa—"

"Tell me!" he screamed.

She held out her palms. "Chaam, you're scaring me. What's going on?"

"The Maaskab sent you, didn't they? You were sent to destroy me."

Maggie choked down the thick lump of dread stuck in her throat. One moment she'd been basking in Chaam's warmth and affection, the next she was lying on the dock, her insides charred. To top it off, she'd woken to a completely different Chaam. This version was cold, furious, and deadly.

Why? And what was this thing—*a maskib?*—he'd accused her of being?

"Get dressed." He tossed the dress to her side. She noticed he now wore his white trousers.

She quickly stood and slipped her dress over her head while her mind bounced against a brick wall. She didn't know what to do. Run perhaps? Something told her that would only make matters worse.

Reason with him. “You need to explain why you are upset.”

“Upset? Gods don’t get upset, Maggie. We get furious, and then we exact our justice.” Terrifying rage flickered in his eyes.

“What did I do?” She stepped back.

“Don’t play stupid. This sort of dark power can only come from one place.” He held up the necklace.

He’s angry over that? “I don’t know what you’re talking about. My father gave it to me.”

“And where did he obtain it? Tell me!” He grabbed her arms. The contact sent tiny shards of hot glass charging through her veins.

She jerked away, gasping in pain. “I don’t know. The ruin, I guess. Why?” She used the air in her lungs to straighten her spine.

He brought his nose to hers and snarled like a monster. “Tell them that they will all burn in hell. The Maaskab will never defeat us. They will never have this world.”

“What are you talking about?” she said.

He stilled for several moments. “Never mind. I will tell them myself. I’m sure your father will know where to find them.”

He turned away and marched off into the jungle.

“No! You’re going to hurt him!” *Oh my God! Oh my God.* “No! Please, please don’t do this!”

She ran after him but found herself alone in the

middle of a stand of trees, without shoes, without knowing where she was going, without knowing how everything had gone so wrong.

She sank to her knees. Why had he turned on her?

Chaam stormed into the brush, pushing down tree after tree to release his anger. How could he have been such a fool? To pathetically believe Maggie was his mate, sent by the universe.

Pathetic fucking fool. Maggie was just an ordinary human with a Maaskab necklace. Well, he surmised it was Maaskab. Those evil bastards had been around since the dawn of the Mayan era. Originally, they had been run-of-the-mill priests. But where there is power to be had, evil always lurks. Centuries of quiet power struggles had eventually led to their outright bloodshed and the decimation of the population. Those who could, escaped, and the Mayan civilization collapsed.

It had been a very dark hour for the gods. They should have intervened; they should have taken the Maaskab down, but their laws prohibited influencing the evolution of humanity unless the path led to complete destruction. At the time, it had not.

Chaam looked toward the early morning sky. Above him perched a black and yellow toucan with a red-tipped beak, staring with needy eyes. "For fuck's sake. Fine! I'll help you with your mate, but you will tell me where to find Maggie's father."

The bird squawked.

The ruin wasn't far. Just a few minutes northwest. "Lead the way, Romeo."

The toucan fluttered off its branch and flew to the next tree and to the next. Chaam's angry march continued along with his mental rant.

Perhaps the Creator didn't exist and there was no such divine intelligence in the universe. Perhaps he and all gods were simply creatures of evolution, instinctually wired to rescue humans. Perhaps there was a way to break this compulsion. Dammit. He deserved to live freely, without the toxic albatross of humanity driving his every move. He was tired of this torment. And now the one brilliant light at the end of his tunnel had been shut off.

Images of Maggie infiltrated his mind, exacerbating his rage. How could she turn out to be Maaskab, of all things?

Chaam's rational mind clicked and began tamping down the barrage of irrational emotions. *Idiot. There are no female Maaskab—only female slaves and sacrificial victims waiting to happen.*

Maggie could never be anything but innocent and loyal.

Fucking hell. How could you accuse her of being a Maaskab? He'd seen her soul. It was pure light.

He stopped in his tracks. "Where the fuck are we?"

The toucan fluttered to a small dirt hill, flapped its colorful wings, and flew off.

To the untrained eye, it appeared as a giant

mound overgrown with vines and small trees. But to one side a dark doorway, about four feet high and three feet wide, stood.

Chaam stared at the entrance for several moments while the gravity of his behavior positioned itself into a stranglehold.

It had been his fear talking earlier. He'd succumbed to it. He'd let it pollute his mind.

Gods dammit. He'd fucked up, plain and simple. Maggie was his destiny. She had been brought into his life to help him find comfort in his eternal role as a deity. And who gave a shit if his ability to touch her and hold her came from a dark Maaskab relic? Dammit. It didn't matter.

Maggie said her father had given her the necklace as a gift. It probably came from this very spot, which might very well be an ancient Maaskab temple. Her father likely thought it was a meaningless rock.

Point was, he could figure all that out later. Fate had brought the necklace to Maggie and Maggie to him.

So why the fuck was he standing there staring at an old decaying ruin? He needed to find her and beg forgiveness. Then he would take her through the cenote and fill her with the light of the gods, making her immortal. The rest could—

A gut-wrenching female scream exploded from the temple.

What the hell? Adrenaline charged through his

humanlike body. He bolted inside only to find an empty, dark, wet chamber corroded with tree roots, spiderwebs, and the dank smell of…

Holy hell. Death. It permeated every wall. And the narrow stairway to the right of the tiny chamber reeked with it. This was the unmistakable scent of Maaskab.

Another scream echoed through the air.

He quietly neared the narrow opening that led to a set of slippery, mold-covered stone steps. With his wide shoulders, he would barely fit into the passage.

The violent scream turned into a muffled moan.

Shit. Chaam squeezed his way down and saw what he'd hoped he would not.

The scrappy-looking man had the tip of a knife buried into the young woman's chest just above her heart. He had tied her to a slab of stone, with a rag jammed in her mouth.

"Let her go," Chaam commanded.

Startled, the man jumped and turned the blade toward Chaam.

Chaam held out his palms. "Dr. O'Hare?"

"Who the hell are you?"

"I know your daughter, Maggie. She sent me to look for you." *Sort of…*

The man tilted his head. "You know my Maggie?"

"Yes. And she's very worried about you. Drop the knife, and we can go find her." Sweat trickled down Chaam's back. He'd never been so nervous in his entire existence. Not when he'd faced an entire army of evil vampires. Not when ten legions of Roman soldiers, hell-bent on slaughtering him and his brother Votan, had barreled down on them. No. Not even then. But now, in this cold, dark chamber, he felt like a sizzling pig on a hot campfire spindle. Maggie's father had gone mad from sorrow; he stank of it. But could Chaam save him? Curing erectile dysfunction was not the same as mending a broken heart, although both were powerful organs that responded well to sex.

"I said drop the fucking knife, you idiot. I'm a god. You can't kill me. At best you'll stick me with the blade, piss me off, and end up dead. Neither of us wants that."

The man stood silent, his wild eyes assessing Chaam. From the smell of it, he hadn't been washed in weeks and neither had his grimy khaki trousers and matching shirt.

"How the hell do you know what I want?" the man finally said.

Funny, he hadn't commented on the god thing. That usually provoked one of two responses in others: They either believed him and became as scared as shit, or they thought he was crazy, which also scared the crap out of them. Neither was the case today.

"Of course I know what you want. Your wife," Chaam replied. "You want her back. But whatever you're doing won't work. By the way, what the hell *are* you doing?"

The man's veins bulged on his wrist and the dagger trembled. "You're wrong. The tablet can bring her back."

Tablet?

Chaam noticed a black tablet the size of a tombstone lying under the woman's head. Likely it was a remnant of some twisted Maaskab decoration.

Chaam nodded. "If what you say is correct, then we will find a way to bring back your wife *without* taking the young woman's life."

The man ran his free hand through his short greasy hair. The torches mounted to the wall flickered, illuminating his dark, empty eyes.

Fuck.

In that brief moment, Chaam peered into the man's soul. *Black. Fucking black.* Not brown. Not gray. Black. No redemption. Kill on the spot. This was law.

Dammit. The man must have been fucking around down there for weeks. Who knew what sort of dark Maaskab bullshit he'd found?

Chaam sucked in a deep breath, hoping that in time his sweet Maggie would heal. And with more time, grow to forgive him.

"Chaam? What's going on?" Maggie's panicked voice echoed through the chamber.

Christ no. "Leave, Maggie!" He did not want to have to execute her father right in front of her.

Confusion swept across her face the moment she registered the sight of her father gripping a large dagger. "Daddy? What are you doing? Why is Itzel tied to that altar?"

Chaam swallowed. She'd obviously just figured out her father was not right. "Maggie, honey, just leave—"

"Don't you dare! Don't you dare call me honey! Not after what you did!"

"What did you do to her?" Her father took one step forward with his trembling knife. "Did you touch my daughter?"

Oh hell. The man was going to attack, and Chaam's mind was ten steps ahead. Step ten, destruction. Him. Maggie. Their hope for a future. It was one thing to kill her father, but it was another to make her watch.

Perhaps he could convince the man to come quietly.

Maggie's father turned away toward the altar, raised the knife, and jerked it toward the young woman's heart. Chaam lunged and caught the knife just in time with one hand. With his other free hand, Chaam wrenched the man's neck. Blood poured from a tear at the base of the man's skull as he fell over the woman on the altar. His red syrupy liquid flowed onto her face and she gurgled in horror, then passed out.

Suddenly, a violent wind kicked up inside the chamber behind him. Chaam watched in terror as a black empty vortex sucked Maggie inside.

"No!" He leapt forward, reaching for Maggie.

Horror filled her face as she reached for him, too, and for a brief moment, their eyes met. So many unspoken words passed between them. She knew Chaam was sorry for what he'd done, and she forgave him. "I love you," her eyes said.

She loves me?

She slid away, disappearing into the darkness.

Wherever she was going, he would join her. He would not pass one second of his existence without her, without being able to tell her he loved her back.

He lunged forward and slammed into a cold, dark wall.

The portal closed.

Chaam's heart turned a million shades of darkness.

Chapter Seven

Sprawled out on the floor, Chaam's head lolled from side to side. Maggie was gone. Maggie was gone. Maggie. Was. Gone. And mind-crippling rage was first on the scene. Self-loathing, the second to arrive. And third…

"Found him!" Cimil stood at the bottom of the steps, happy as an evil clam, pointing at Maggie's father's lifeless body.

"Fucking hell, Cimil," he groaned.

"Wow." She rolled her head and surveyed the room. "Looks like you had quite the shin-diggedy-dig party. Didn't know bloodbaths were back in fashion. Personally, I'm tired of mud, so yippy! It's my lucky day!"

She was always so damned evil. And late. "Where the hell have you been?"

"I stopped to have this frock-o-licious ensemble made. And by *made*, I mean I stole it." She now wore an elaborately beaded white dress. "My mariachi suit was a loaner, and el Señor Trumpet had a wedding gig. But lucky me, I found this. Boy, did that bride look pissed. Maybe Señor Trumpet will loan her his outfit." She grinned. "So, you need some help, yes?"

He scraped himself up off the grimy, blood-soaked floor and charged. She moved to the side, away from his open claw, but wasn't fast enough. He slammed her against the wall. "Fuck you. This is your fault. You were supposed to find Maggie's father."

"Yeah. Funny you should mention that," she grunted. "I actually took a peekee-poo into the future and saw all paths led to this one. No escape."

He released her. "What are you saying?"

Cimil rubbed her neck. "This was Fate's plan all along. You were meant to lose Maggie."

Her words crushed his very soul. "No. This can't be right. Fate wants me to suffer?"

"Yep! But there are many paths forward potentially ending in your happiness."

He braced his two arms against the wall next. The air no longer wanted to enter his lungs, but the darkness did. This entire place was saturated with it, and his agony only seemed to amplify the potency. No wonder Maggie's father had turned evil. But there might still be hope for himself. Maybe. He wanted to fight. "What do you mean?"

"What I mean is I can reunite you with your precious mortal."

Could she? Cimil was known for her deception. That said, she *was* the Goddess of the Underworld. Her powers were an enigma, even to the gods.

"How?" he asked.

"Simple." Cimil gyrated her hips.

Un-fucking-believable. "Are you dancing?"

Still circling her hips and staring off into space, she replied, "Uh-uh. I've got a hula hoop contest tonight. I'm gonna win this time. I can feeeel it!"

Chaam raised his open hand. "I don't know what a hula hoop is, but you're not winning shit without your head."

She stopped her strange little dance and then rolled her eyes. "Fine! I will prevent Margaret from crossing over into the eternal light of the universe, where she would be recycled—perhaps into a tree or a bullfrog or a chicken potpie. Or a very naughty clown. One never knows. Then we will find a way to reunite the two of you."

"Are you telling me she's...she's..." A black cloud besieged him, and in that moment, the invisible shackles that had compelled him to protect the mortal world for thousands of years snapped. Every. Single. Fucking. One of them.

"Maggie is dead?" Chaam sank down. He'd never imagined such emptiness and despair could exist inside him. It was like a cancer fed by his rage. A rage that would never cease until he had her back.

He now understood the true meaning of torment. He now understood Maggie's father.

"Tell me what to do," he mumbled.

"How far are you willing to go?" Cimil crouched in front of him. A sinister twinkle gleamed in her eyes.

"I would do anything."

"Peachy! There are two options. One, you reopen the portal with the tablet—good luck with that, by the way—it's nearly impossible."

"Impossible?"

"Yes. Impossible. As in almost never, ever, ever, ever, ever, ever, ever, ever...ever!"

"I just opened it."

"Ah! But you see, it only opens once every ten or so cycles on the Day of the Dead, when the sun is just so in the sky and a tiny frog hops from one lily pad to the next just as he's gulping down a fly born precisely twenty-six hours earlier when the temperature of the air is exactly seventy-two point three degrees and the wind blows at five miles per hour due east, just—and I mean just!—as a man with a black soul is nearly decapitated by a deity who is in love with his daughter, and the blood pours on a virgin lying directly over the tablet, on an altar at the mouth of a giant black jade cave." Cimil sucked in a deep breath and then scratched the corner of her mouth. "Or something *like* that. But I can't be sure."

Did she think this was one of her fucking little games?

Chaam threw Cimil against the slimy stone wall and clamped his hand around her neck. Her legs dangled several feet above the ground. "Stop. Fucking. With me," he growled.

"I don't know what you mean," she croaked.

"Tell me! How do I reopen the portal?" He knocked her against the wall several times.

"I told you! It's some mystical algorithm—planets aligning, virgins, blood, tiny creatures eating… You heard me!"

He thumped her against the wall once more.

She pointed at the altar. "I'm telling the truth. Look at the tablet! The instructions are right there in Maaskabese. If you can decipher it, you can go anywhere! Backward, forward, side to side, the other side, the outlet stores. Even The Rack. Fabulous, right?"

He released her, and she slid down the wall like butter on a heap of hot pancakes.

Chaam moved to the altar where the young woman—Maggie had called her Itzel, he thought—lay unconscious, bathed in blood—not hers, thankfully. He slid the tablet out from beneath her head and examined the shimmering black artifact. "Black granite?"

"Jade. From the mine." Cimil pointed to an opening about four feet in diameter under the stairs. "It's powerful stuff. I think you'll find it…useful for what comes next."

Chaam's eyes made a quick sweep. "This is an entrance to a mine?"

Cimil nodded. "The Maaskab's best kept secret."

His attention moved back to the tablet. The writing appeared to be Mayan, but he did not recognize the symbols. "What does it say?"

"I told you what I know."

Perhaps she told the truth, perhaps not. But he'd known Cimil for seventy thousand years, and whatever information she might have, she wasn't going to share. Yet.

"What's the second option?" he asked.

"Oh boy. After the wall-thumping you just gave me, not sure I want to go there."

"Tell me!"

"Okaaay, but it's big. It's bad. It's glamorous and icky. Are you suuure you're willing to do anything to get her back?"

"I'd tear apart the whole fucking world stone by fucking stone."

"Oh goody!" Cimil jumped up and down, clapping. "This really is my lucky day! Because that is exactly what I had in mind!"

Why would she want that? She hadn't been singled out by the universe for this cruel, horrible fate, for this unbearable, unjust punishment.

"What's in this for you, Cimil?"

Her face turned into a tundra of icy starkness. She grabbed him by the arms and sent paralyzing shock waves of searing pain through his system. "See, brother. See into my eyes. See what the dead have shown me."

Chaam leaned down and met her gaze, but he would find no visions of the dead. *Not today*, she thought.

"Let the darkness in, brother," Cimil commanded with hypnotic waves that burrowed into the depths of his soul. "That's a good boy. Just let it in. Think of your precious Maggie, of how much you love her and how she was so cruelly ripped away. Yes, that's right. Let all that pain in. Feel the darkness consume you."

"Yes," he said with a vacant stare to match his vacant heart. "I will let the darkness in. I understand now."

Cimil sighed, pushed her head to his chest, and embraced him with teary eyes. "There will be much suffering ahead, brother. And for this, I am sorry," she whispered. "But I promise, when this is all over, your soul will be washed clean and Maggie will be waiting for you."

Gods, she hoped. This journey would not be an easy one and could backfire a million different ways. One wrong turn, one mistake, and her plan would go up in a not-so-dramatastic cloud of smoke. Boom. Dead. Everyone. But the dead had shown her what was to come, and there was no choice but to march forward. In the meantime...

She'd always loved doing bad things! Now was her chance to truly enjoy it—vicariously through Chaam, of course! Because unlike her, his deity-do-gooder bond with the universe had broken.

Cimil released him. "Fabulous! You're going to have so much fun! Evil is the new good! We'll pretend it's a game—'kay? Evil Cimi Says."

"When do we start?" he murmured.

"No time like the present," she said. "Let's go find some evil Maaskab and have an evil chat."

Epilogue

Approximately Eighty Years Later

Blood trickled from Maggie's pale clenched fists as she stared at Chaam's shivering body through the dense smoky film separating her from the physical world. Too many years she'd watched helplessly as he suffered. His incarceration was a hell no living being should have to endure. "Hang on, my love. This will all soon be over."

Maggie knew from the moment she'd entered this realm that she would find a way out. And when she did, there would be hell to pay. Because while Cimil had orchestrated her chaos, forcing Chaam to commit vile, evil acts in the name of her sick and twisted amusement, Maggie had been watching, listening, and learning the gods' tricks and secrets. And with the scalpel-sharp precision of a vengeful, mad surgeon, Maggie tweaked and manipulated and pulled and tugged on every invisible string within her grasp until the tides of fate had eventually shifted.

"Please don't give up, Chaam. Please. I'm almost free, and soon, you will be, too. Don't give up." She needed him to hang on to that last piece of his soul just a little longer. Without it, he would be lost forever. If only he could hear her and know she was there. *Just this once. Just this once. Please hear me just this once…*

She threw back her head to fight the tears and gazed up at the pristine blue sky—it was her favorite mirage. Anything that reminded her of Bacalar and her time with Chaam gave her comfort.

"Please come soon, bobcat. I cannot hold on for much longer."

Maggie gasped.

TO BE CONTINUED…

AUTHOR'S NOTE

Hi, All!

I hope you enjoyed reading this extra little piece of the Accidentally Yours Series that continues on with *VAMPIRES NEED NOT...APPLY?* (Book 4). AND! After you've finished this series, if you're looking for more Cimil and her crazy gang, don't forget to check out their NEW stories in the IMMORTAL MATCHMAKERS, INC. SERIES! (At the moment, I'm working on Book 4, *THE GODDESS OF FORGETFULNESS.*)

FREE BOOKMARKS:
As always, I have FREE signed bookmarks for my readers.
EMAIL me at: mimi@mimijean.net.
Please DO MENTION if you've posted a review so I can thank you and possibly throw in an extra-goody from my swag stash. (First come basis. International OK.)

WHERE TO HANG OUT WITH ME ON LINE?
Join my group on Facebook!
facebook.com/groups/MimiJeansJunkies

Or, if you just want new release alerts, sign up for my sorta-kinda-monthly newsletter:

Sign up for Mimi's mailing list for giveaways and new release news!

Happy reading!
Hugs,
Mimi

STALK MIMI:
www.mimijean.net
twitter.com/MimiJeanRomance
pinterest.com/mimijeanromance
instagram.com/mimijeanpamfiloff
facebook.com/MimiJeanPamfiloff

THE IMMORTAL MATCHMAKERS

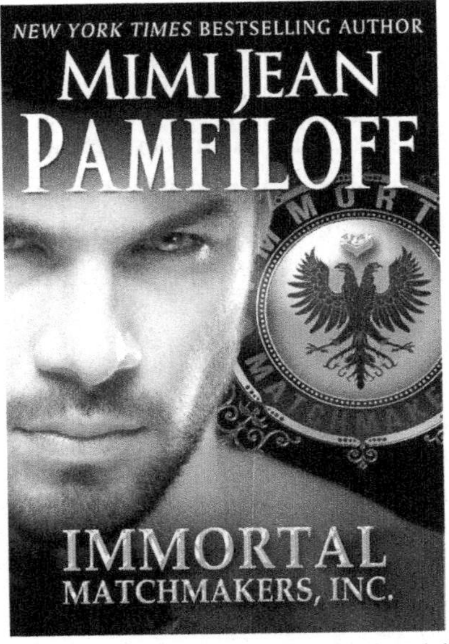

Because dysfunctional immortals need love, too.

SEVEN DAYS TO GO FROM LETHAL IMMORTAL ASSASSIN TO PRINCE CHARMING. DOES HE STAND A CHANCE?

Demigod Andrus Gray may look like every woman's dream, but when it comes to charm, he sees no point in pretending: He has none and makes no apologies for it. Behaving nicely hasn't made him the deadly assassin he is today. But is that really the reason he's still single?

The Goddess Cimil—owner of Immortal Matchmakers, Inc.—thinks yes. So when she foresees a mate in Andrus's near future, she's determined to make the match happen. That means hiring aspiring actress Sadie Townsend to help the barbarian "act" a little more civilized.

But are seven days really enough? And why does he suddenly have the urge to throw away an eternity of love for just one night with Sadie?

Excerpt – The Immortal Matchmakers

CHAPTER ONE

"Godsdammit. I'm going to need a snack." Zac, God of Temptation and the most awesome mother-fucking badass deity on the planet, took his Bionic Man lunchbox from his black leather backpack, placed it on his desk, and went for his bologna sandwich.

"Fuck. Me. This can't be happening," he whispered and tore off a big bite while staring at the computer screen. *One hundred and fifty?* They hadn't even been open for a day.

His computer made that strange little swoosh sound, indicating more of this "email" crap was flowing into his "inbox."

He took another bite and nearly choked. "What the bloody hell?" Now two hundred and eighty immortals had filled out the online request form.

He looked over his shoulder, across the empty space of the twentieth floor, which they'd rented in downtown L.A. The big corner office remained empty.

Traitor.

It was well past noon, yet his crazy fucking red-headed mess of a sister Cimil, The Goddess of the Underworld, was nowhere to be found on their official first day of business. Of course, she'd insisted on getting the only office because she was "critical to mankind's survival."

What a bunch of deity-crap. As far as he was concerned, they were both equally valuable to humanity and both in this mess for two reasons: One, she was bat-shit crazy. And two, he'd trusted her. Having to open this matchmaking agency for immortals was all her goddamned fault.

That's right. My only crime was falling in love with my brother's woman. Yeah, so maybe he'd crossed a few lines, using his powers to try (and fail) to break them up. But banishment by the other gods to this hellhole of traffic, smog, and heat they called "Los Angeles"? Then having to come to this enormous, soul-sucking coffin of glass and steel—called an "office building"—every day to work like some lowly mortal slave to assist the unlaid immortal masses?

No fucking gracias, amigos.

His eyes darted around the empty space, taking note of its tragically undignified decorum of white walls, gray carpet, and artificial lighting. *Maybe I can spruce up the place with some paintings of naked women and chocolate—tempting shit like that.*

He shoved the rest of his sandwich into his mouth, dusted off his hands on his black leather pants, and went back to his computer, toggling through the profiles. *Vampire, vampire, demigod, my brother, my other brother, Uchben, immortal warrior…unicorn?*

"Hi. Are you Zac?" said a sweet, feminine voice.

He looked up and found a short woman with a long blonde ponytail and big blue eyes, standing in the doorway, looking very nervous. Her petite body, though covered in a horribly unrevealing dress with disgusting flowers all over it, was cute and curvy.

She batted her big blues in question.

He held up his index finger and swallowed down the lump of food. "Yeah, I'm Zac. Who the hell are you?" She appeared human, but this was a matchmaking agency for immortals only.

With an eager, friendly smile she approached, holding out her hand. "I'm Tula Jones. So nice to meet you."

He stood from his chair and watched her gaze follow his face up, up, up.

Her mouth fell open. "She wasn't lying; you really are big."

Of course. He was a deity—one of fourteen, over seventy thousand years old, and seven feet of masculine perfection right down to his godsdamned dingle berries. Not that he had any, because he was far too perfect for that shit.

Zac crossed his powerful arms over his magnificent chest. "Yes, I am big. In many, many ways." He cocked a suggestive brow, wondering how many seconds it would take her to reach out and touch him. The ladies always wanted a little feel. "So which lucky lady sent you?" It wasn't uncommon for the women to talk after an exquisite night with him. A god. A badass god. With a huge cock. And he'd been plowing a whole hell of a lot of mortal fields these past few weeks. Hell, what else was there to do? Cry over his broken, banished, badass heart? No fucking way.

"Uh, well," she said meekly, "your sister Cimil told me about you. Said I shouldn't be afraid or let you push me around."

Cimil sent me a woman to fuck? This Tula was a bit small for his taste, around five feet or so, but she looked like she might know her way around a cock. Maybe this day was looking up.

"She hired me to be your assistant," Tula added, her nervous eyes continuing to scale up and down his body.

Oh. So no afternoon booty delivery, huh? Maybe he'd go next door to the Starbucks and pick someone up. Banished and powerless or not, he was still a deity and completely irresistible to women. What his body didn't catch, his scent did. One whiff and the ladies swarmed like horny bees.

"And what makes my sister think I need an assistant?" he said skeptically.

"Your sister said, and I quote, 'He is a giant

asshat and completely useless, so he needs someone to do everything for him.'"

He wasn't an asshat. An asshole, maybe. But either way, was Cimil out of her immortal skull? Humans were on a need-to-know basis because they usually freaked the fuck out about the immortal community. They'd have everything from vampires to that nightmare of a head case, Cimil's unicorn, coming through on a daily basis.

Tula added, "She also mentioned that you might need some cheering up and moral support. And, wow, she was right about your hair."

"My hair?" He ran his hand over the length of his shaggy black mane.

"She said it screamed depression. Want me to book you a salon appointment?" Tula asked.

What? His hair did not scream "depression." It looked shiny and unkempt and screamed "badass!" The women constantly complimented him on how it set off his turquoise eyes.

Of course, they're usually looking at the bulge in my pants when they say it.

"I'm sorry," he said, growling, "but I think there's been a mistake. We're not hiring."

"Uh-huh," Tula said cheerily. "Should I sit here?" She walked around the desk and slid her petite frame past his body, sending a hard spike of arousal through his groin. She took the seat he'd just been in and looked up at him, smiling sassily.

"What are you doing?" he said.

"Your sister also explained that you'd try to run me off. Because, and I quote, 'He's a giant asshat and thinks he's too awesome to need help from anyone.'"

He growled and reached for her. "Okay, little girl, it's time for you—"

She leaned away from his hand. "Please don't kick me out. I really need this job."

He froze and then dropped his hand. *Godsdammit.* "My sister told you to say that, didn't she?"

Tula shook her head. "No. But it's the truth. I need the money for college. I've only got one more year left, and my parents can't afford the tuition. This is the only job I've been able to find that comes close to paying the bills and is flexible enough for me to go to school."

Bloody fucking hell. She'd found his loophole. No, he didn't mean his asshole—his loophole. A deity's purpose was to help humans. It was hardwired into their DNA from day one.

Now he had to help.

He scratched his unshaven jaw, unsure of what to do with her. Why would Cimil hire this naïve little human female to help them pay their penance—finding mates for one hundred immortals—or something like that? Honestly, the other garble the other gods had said at his sentencing about learning compassion and the true meaning of love had gone in one ear and out the other. The part about being stripped of his powers and banished, however? Well, that stuck like dog shit on a shoe.

"Fine," he grumbled. "You can stay. But just for the time being until you find another job."

"Thank you! Thank you," she said. "I promise you won't be disappointed. I'm a hard worker and great at organizing."

"Yes. Yes. You're welcome. You're welcome," he said blandly. Now where would he sit? He looked around the empty room that would also serve as their lobby. "I'll work in there." *Fuck Cimil.* She hadn't shown, so he'd take the big office. Let her sit on the floor. "Maybe you can start by ordering some…" He waved his hand in the air. "Some things to make this hellhole look less like a hell-hole." Gods only knew how long he'd have to keep coming here; might as well make it worthy of a deity.

"Okay. I'll get right on it." She glanced down at the desk. "Is that a Bionic Man lunch pail?"

"Yes." *Silly mortal.* Could she not see the giant letters on the metal box, clearly stating "The Bionic Man"?

"My dad had one of those when he was little. A huge Bionic Man fan," she said.

Her father? But the woman at the very "cool and hip" store for younger humans had said that it was what the "edgy" and "fucking awesome" people used these days to transport their afternoon meals. No, he didn't have to eat but enjoyed doing it anyway. Yes, he was a stress eater. Okay? Even deities had their challenges. *Thankfully, I don't gain weight. I'm just a giant piece of awesome.*

Zac looked down at the lunch box and rubbed his jaw. "Well, it's a…a friend gave it to me as a joke." *Note to badass self: Must smite salesperson at trendy store for deceiving me.*

"Aww…well, I think it's cute," she said.

In that case, I will merely maim salesperson.

Tula scooted her body closer to the desk. "So, where would you like me to start after I order the furniture?" She flashed a smile that, despite its nervousness, was bright and cheery. Of course, that happy shit was completely lost on him.

"Ehhh…well, what exactly did my sister tell you?"

"Um, that you are the God of Temptation—now exiled and powerless—and she is the Goddess of the Underworld, also exiled, though she still communes with the dead. She is also a new mother to two boys and two girls, and, I quote, 'one dangerous mess of woman-hormones with giant cow udders.'"

"She told you what we are?" he asked. "And you're not afraid?"

She shook her head, her blonde ponytail flopping side to side. "No, sir. My momma raised me with an open mind, and I always suspected there was more to this world than what I saw with my eyes." She shrugged. "I love being right."

Funny. Me too!

"Ah, well. In that case, Tula, welcome to reality."

She leaned forward, lacing her hands together. "So is it true? You have an army of immortal warriors, kind of like the bad vampires in the *Twilight* book?"

He cringed. "We are gods. Fourteen of the most powerful creatures in existence, not…" He made a sour face. "Vampires." Of course, in general he didn't have anything against those sneaky sifting bastards. For example, his brother Kinich, ex-God of the Sun, was now a vampire, and even Cimil's mate, Roberto, was an Ancient One—the first of his kind. He was also once an Egyptian pharaoh, which made him an arrogant, ruthless fucker. Who could resist liking that?

He added, "We are divine, my dear human. Birthed from the Universe's womb."

She shrugged. "I still loved *Twilight*."

He gave her a look and was about to speak when he noticed something unexpected: Her aura.

Holy fuck. What. Is. That? In his seventy thousand years, he'd never seen a human with a purer soul. Not one. Looking at her was like gazing at a patch of newly fallen snow.

"You okay, Mr. Zac?" she asked.

He nodded dumbly.

"'Cause you look like you want to put whatever you just ate right back in the Bionic Man box." She scooted the lunch pail closer to him.

I've done for you," she squabbled.

"You mean the fact that I'm being punished because you lied and manipulated me?" She'd promised everything would work out with his brother's woman if he followed her advice. Of course, Cimil claimed everything *had* worked out. Just not for him.

"Exactly." She shrugged happily. "And stop your whining. I got banished, too, and the only thing I did was tell a few lies, torture a few innocent souls, and save the world from ending. How fair is that?"

"Uh, because you were secretly driving the world to its end at the same time?" Of course, she couldn't really help it. Like him, she had her dark side, but ultimately served the greater good. Very twisted.

That Universe and her sense of humor. What a riot.

"Now shoo!" She swept her hands through the air. "Minky needs her rest."

Zac shook his head. Minky was Cimil's pet, a bloodthirsty and invisible unicorn. It was better not to speak of such things.

He followed Cimil out, and she closed the door behind her and locked it. "Okay. I have my womba class—boy, those four little monsters really stretched the old uterus right out—then Roberto and I have our daddy-vampire and mommy-goddess class. See you both tomorrow."

Zac was about to ask about the class, but then realized he didn't give a fuck.

"Tootles!" Cimil said, wiggling her pale gaunt fingers in the air. "And keep your paws off Tula! She's taken!"

Dammit, Cimil. She knew that saying that would make him want her more. He hoped she was joking about the taken part.

"Wait," he said. "You never told me who our first 'in the bag' client is."

She flashed a devilish grin over her shoulder. "The infamous Andrus Gray."

Oh, hell. That guy? Definitely not in the bag. "If that's the case, then we are going to need his best friend's help."

Glossary

Black Jade – Found only in a particular mine located in southern Mexico, this jade has very special supernatural properties, including the ability to absorb supernatural energy—in particular, god energy. When worn by humans, it is possible for them to have physical contact with a god. If injected, it can make a person addicted to doing bad things. If the jade is fueled with dark energy and then released, it can be used as a weapon. Chaam, personally, likes using it to polish his teeth.

The Book of the Oracle of Delphi – This mystical text from 1400 BC is said to have been created by one of the great oracles at Delphi and can tell the future. As the events in present time change the future, the book's pages magically rewrite themselves. The demigods use this book in Book 2 to figure out when and how to kill the Vampire Queen. Helena also reads it while they're captive, and learns she must sacrifice her mortality to save Niccolo.

Cenote – Limestone sinkholes connected to a subterranean water system. They are found in Central America and southern Mexico and were once believed by the Maya to be sacred portals to the afterlife. Such smart humans! They were right. Except, cenotes are actually portals to the realm of the gods.

(If you have never seen a cenote, do a quick search on the internet for "cenote photos," and you'll see how freaking cool they are!)

Demilords – (Spoiler alert for Book 2!) This is a group of immortal badass vampires who've been infused with the light of the gods. They are extremely difficult to kill and hate their jobs (killing Obscuros) almost as much as they hate the gods who control them.

Maaskab – Originally a cult of bloodthirsty Mayan priests who believed in the dark arts. It is rumored they are responsible for bringing down their entire civilization with their obsession for human sacrifices (mainly young female virgins). Once Chaam started making half-human children, he decided all firstborn males would make excellent Maaskab due to their proclivity for evil.

Mocos, Mobscuros, O'scabbies – Nicknames for when you join Maaskab with Obscuros to create a brand new malevolent treat.

Obscuros – Evil vampires who do not live by the Pact and who like to dine on innocent humans since they really do taste the best.

The Pact – An agreement between the gods and good vampires that dictates the dos and don'ts. There are many parts to it, but the most important rules are: Vampires are not allowed to snack on good people (called Forbiddens), they must keep their existence a secret, and they are responsible for keeping any rogue vampires in check.

Payal – Although the gods can take humans to their realm and make them immortal, Payals are the true genetic offspring of the gods but are born mortal, just like their human mothers. Only firstborn children inherit the gods' genes and manifest their traits. If the firstborn happens to be female, she is a Payal. If male, well…then you get something kind of yucky (see definition of Maaskab)!

Uchben – An ancient society of scholars and warriors who serve as the gods' eyes and ears in the human world. They also do the books and manage the gods' earthly assets.

Character Definitions

The Gods

Although every culture around the world has their own names and beliefs related to beings of worship, there are actually only fourteen gods. And since the gods are able to access the human world only through the portals called cenotes, located in the Yucatan, the Maya were big fans.

The gods often refer to each other as brother and sister, but the truth is they are just another species of the Creator.

1. Acan – God of Wine and Intoxication. Also known as Belch, Acan has been drunk for a few thousand years. He hopes to someday trade places with Votan because he's tired of his flabby muscles and beer belly.

2. Ah-Ciliz – God of Solar Eclipses. Called A.C. by his brethren, Ah-Ciliz is generally thought of as the party-pooper because of his dark attitude.

3. Akna – Goddess of Fertility. You either love her or you hate her.

4. Backlum Chaam – God of Male Virility. He's responsible for discovering black jade, figuring out how to procreate with humans, and kicking off the chain of events that will eventually lead to the Great War. Get your Funyuns and beer! This is gonna be good.

5. Camaxtli – Goddess of the Hunt. Also known as Fate, Camaxtli holds a special position among the gods, since no one dares challenge her. When Fate has spoken, that's the end of the conversation.

6. Colel Cab – Mistress of Bees. Because, really, where would we all be without the bees?

7. Goddess of Forgetfulness – Um…I forget her name. Sorry.

8. Ixtab – Goddess of Suicide. Ixtab is generally described as a loner. Could it be those dead critters she carries around? But don't judge her so hastily. You never know what truly lies behind that veil of black she wears.

9. K'ak – The history books remember him as K'ak Tiliw Chan Yopaat, ruler of Copán in the 700s AD. King K'ak (Don't you just love that name? Tee hee hee…) is one of Cimil's favorite brothers. We're not really sure what he does, but he can throw bolts of lightning.

10. Kinich Ahau – God of the Sun. Also known by many other names, depending on the culture,

Kinich likes to go by "Nick" these days. But don't let the modern name fool you. He's not so hot about the gods mingling with humans. Although...he's getting a little curious about what the fuss is all about. Can sleeping with a woman really be all that?

11. Votan – God of Death and War. Also known as Odin, Wotan, Wodan, God of Drums (he has no idea how the hell he got that title; he hates the drums), and God of Multiplication (okay, he is pretty darn good at math, so that one makes sense). These days, Votan goes by Guy Santiago (it's a long story—read Book 1), but despite his deadly tendencies, he's all heart. He's now engaged to Emma Keane.

12. Yum Cimil – Goddess of the Underworld, also known as Ah-Puch by the Maya, Mictlantecuhtli (try saying that one ten times) by the Aztecs, Grim Reaper by the Europeans, Hades by the Greeks...you get the picture! Despite what people say, Cimil is actually a female, adores a good bargain (especially garage sales), and the color pink. She's also bat-shit crazy.

13. Zac Cimi – Bacab of the North. What the heck is a Bacab? According to the gods' folklore, the Bacabs are the four eldest and most powerful of the gods. Zac, however, has yet to discover his true gifts, although he is physically the strongest. We *think* he may be the god of love.

14. ??? (I'm not telling.)

Not the Gods

Andrus – Ex-demilord (vampire who's been given the gods' light), now just a demigod after his maker, the vampire queen, died. According to Cimil, his son, who hasn't been born yet, is destined to marry Helena and Niccolo's daughter.

Anne – Not telling.

Brutus – One of Gabrán's elite Uchben warriors. He doesn't speak much, but that's because he and his team are telepathic. They are also immortal (a gift from the gods) and next in line to be Uchben chiefs.

Emma Keane – A reluctant Payal who can split a man right down the middle with her bare hands. She is engaged to Votan (aka Guy Santiago) and really wants to kick the snot out of Tommaso, the man who betrayed her.

Father Xavier – Once a priest at the Vatican, Xavier is now the Uchben's top scholar and historian. He has a thing for jogging suits, Tyra Banks, and Cimil.

Gabrán – One of the Uchben chiefs and a very close friend of the gods. The chiefs have been given the gods' light and are immortal—a perk of the job.

Gabriela – Emma Keane's grandmother and one of the original Payals. She now leads the Maaskab at the young age of eightysomething.

Helena Strauss – Once human, Helena is now a vampire and married to Niccolo DiConti. She has a half-vampire daughter, Matty, who is destined to marry Andrus's son, according to Cimil.

Jess – Not telling.

Julie Trudeau – Penelope's mother.

Niccolo Di Conti – Ex-general of the vampire queen's army. He is the interim vampire leader now that the queen is dead, because the army remained loyal to him. He is married to Helena Strauss and has a half-vampire daughter, Matty—a wedding gift from Cimil.

Nick – (From Book 1, not to be confused with Kinich). Also not telling.

Penelope Trudeau – The woman Cimil approaches to be her brother's surrogate.

Philippe – Roberto's brother. An Ancient One.

Reyna – The dead vampire queen.

Roberto (Narmer)— Originally an Egyptian pharaoh, Narmer was one of the six Ancient Ones—the very first vampires. He eventually changed his name to Roberto and moved to Spain—something to do with one of Cimil's little schemes. Rumor is, he wasn't too happy about it.

Sentin – One of Niccolo's loyal vampire soldiers. Viktor turned him into a vampire after finding him in a ditch during WWII.

Tommaso – Oh boy. Where to start. Once an Uchben, Tommaso's mind was poisoned with black jade. He tried to kill Emma. She's not happy about that.

Viktor – Niccolo's right hand and BFF. He's approximately one thousand years old and originally a Viking. He's big. He's blond. He's got the hots for some blonde woman he's dreamed of for the last five hundred years. He's also Helena's maker.

2018 RELEASES
THE GODDESS OF FORGETFULNESS

She's spent her whole life hoping to be remembered.

Until him…

www.mimijean.net/forgetty.html

SKINNY PANTS
BOOK 4, THE HAPPY PANTS SERIES

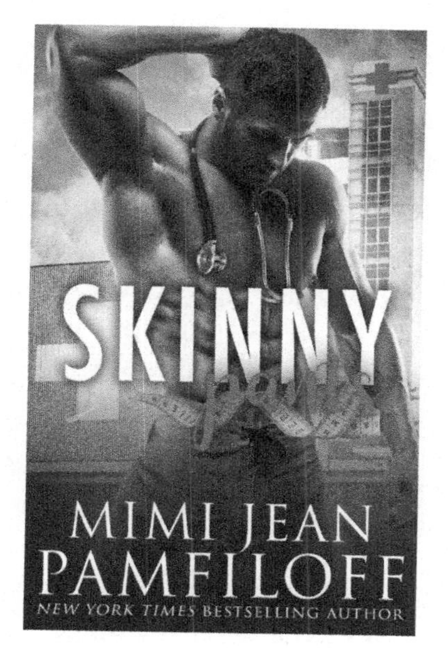

He's the doctor of her dreams.

She's got room to lose.

But this plump ER nurse will have to face facts:

A solid relationship begins when you're ready to take it all off.

www.mimijean.net/skinny-pants.html

DIGGING A HOLE

He's the meanest boss ever.
She's the sweet shy intern.
They're about to wreck each other crazy.

My name is Sydney Lucas. I am smart, deathly shy, and one hundred percent determined to make my own way in the world. Which is why I jumped at the chance to intern for Mr. Nick Brooks despite his reputation. After ten failed interviews at other companies, he was the only one offering. Plus, everyone says he knows his stuff, and surely a man as stunningly handsome as him can't be "the devil incarnate," right? Wrong.

Oh…that man. That freakin' man has got to go! I've been on the job one week, and he's insulted my mother, wardrobe shamed me, and managed to make me cry. Twice. Underneath that stone-cold, beautiful face is the evilest human being ever.

But I'm not going to quit. Oh no. For once in my life, I've got to make a stand. Only, every time I open my mouth, I can't quite seem to muster the courage. Perhaps my revenge needs to come in another form: destroying him quietly.

Because I've got a secret. I'm not really just an intern, and Sydney Lucas isn't my real name.

ABOUT THE AUTHOR

San Francisco native MIMI JEAN PAMFILOFF is a *New York Times* bestselling romance author. Although she obtained her MBA and worked for more than fifteen years in the corporate world, she believes that it's never too late to come out of the romance closet and follow your dream. Mimi now lives with her Latin lover hubby, two pirates-in-training (their boys), and the rat terrier duo, Snowflake and Mini Me, in Arizona. She hopes to make you laugh when you need it most and continues to pray daily that leather pants will make a big comeback for men.

Sign up for Mimi's mailing list for giveaways and new release news!

STALK MIMI:
www.mimijean.net
twitter.com/MimiJeanRomance
pinterest.com/mimijeanromance
instagram.com/mimijeanpamfiloff
facebook.com/MimiJeanPamfiloff

Made in the USA
Coppell, TX
11 November 2021